Miss Agnes and the Ginger Tom

Kirkpatrick Hill

For Lou Honderich,
practically perfect in every way.

Chapter 1

Sam White kidnapped Miss Agnes for us.

He's the one who flies in our mail, Sam. In his Gullwing Stinson. Miss Agnes was going back to England because she'd been teaching upriver for a long time. And because the war was over, that one when England got bombed. And because she missed England a lot.

She was almost on the big plane in Fairbanks when Sam kidnapped her because we needed a teacher.

When he brought her to us we were so surprised because she wasn't like any of the other teachers.

For one thing, she wore pants. Around here women and us girls wear dresses and our moccasins and those thick tan socks that don't stay up very good. We never saw a woman wear pants before.

And for another thing, she didn't talk very much. All the other teachers talked so much after awhile we forgot to listen. Miss Agnes always said things in the shortest way. Like our grandma.

When we're doing something Grandma doesn't like she just says "*kkaa*" in this hard kind of way. That's Indian for stop it. And we do stop it, because Grandma is not anyone you want to fool around with.

Sometimes Miss Agnes just said things with her face, especially with her eyebrows. Or with her whole head, just nod her head for no, or yes, or tilt her head sideways to ask a question. You see? Not a lot of talking.

Miss Agnes never got mad, or was bossy, and she didn't talk that kind of teacher talk, high and fakey. She just talked real. And she talked the way English people talk, without any r's, for another thing.

She didn't do *anything* like other teachers did. Like grades. Or tests. And she didn't like desks in a row.

Everything was always so interesting and different that even everyone who never liked school at all loved it with Miss Agnes.

We had a hard time to get our school because our village was so small, we didn't have enough kids. That's what grandpa says. But Marie's mamma had a whole bunch of kids one right after another, and Roger's mom, too, so then after awhile we had enough. We made a school in Old Man Johnson's cabin right by the river because he was dead and no one lived in it anymore. That was when I was six.

Before Miss Agnes we had a hard time with teachers. We had a lot of them. They sometimes didn't stay the whole year, and some of them cried a lot, and even if they stayed the whole year they never came back. Just too far away from anything, Grandpa said, and too cold in the winter, and stuff like that. Just not used to it.

Then Sam White kidnapped Miss Agnes for us when our last teacher left after only a month.

We knew all along Miss Agnes would only stay one year, because Sam only kidnapped her for a year, and we were so sad about that. We were sad about it all year, even before she was gone in the spring. I didn't know you could miss someone when they were still there.

After school was over Miss Agnes left and then me and Bokko and Mamma and Grandpa and Grandma went to fish camp like we always do.

Me and Bokko spent all summer at fish camp getting used to the idea that Miss Agnes wouldn't be there when we got back, and we always had that hurting feeling when we thought about all the good times that were gone.

And then the night we came back from fish camp me and Bokko stood out in the dark and rain and looked into the school because there was a lamp shining in there. The new teacher, we thought. But there she was, our Miss Agnes that we thought was gone forever.

And a *cat*.

Bokko and I hardly slept all night we were so excited. And then when we finally fell asleep we slept too long.

Bertha, that's my best friend, came to get me and Bokko before we even had our clothes on, and Bertha could hardly stand still. Bertha and her family and everyone else in the village had come back from fish camp before us, so they all knew about Miss Agnes coming back.

"Guess what!" she said as soon as she came in the door.

"We know," I said.

"Well, guess what else," she said.

"She brought a cat," I said.

Bertha looked a little crabby that we knew that. In our village everyone likes to be the first one to tell the news.

"We saw them last night through the window," I said.

"Well, hurry," she said. "Hurry!" She signed two hurries in a row, really fast, for Bokko. Bokko is deaf and all of us sign to her, not very good sometimes, but she knows usually what we mean.

Even Mamma was almost smiling that we were so

silly-happy, and she didn't get mad that we hardly ate our breakfast. I think Mamma was really glad about Miss Agnes coming back. But before Miss Agnes came Mamma thought school was useless.

Miss Agnes had given me her little fat brown tea pot when she left in the spring. To remember her with.

I took it down from the shelf and told Mamma, "She'll need this again."

We all ran to the school as soon as Bokko and I were dressed. We were in such a hurry we just ran through the puddles and didn't care about the splashes so when we got there we were just wet and muddy.

All the other kids were at school ahead of us, sitting in their same old desks, and they turned their heads to look at us when we came in, their eyes all happy. They wanted to see our faces when we saw Miss Agnes.

Roger and Little Pete and Jimmy Sam are the big boys in our school and there's one big girl, Marie. Then me and Bertha and Kenny and Plasker are the middle ones. Bertha's eleven like me, and Kenny and Plasker are too, because that year everyone had a lot of babies. And Toby Joe, I almost forgot. Toby Joe's the same age as Bokko and Bokko is two years older than me. And Selina and Charlie-Boy are the littlest, but this year Toby Joe's little brother Benny was old enough for school. So that makes thirteen of us and those others were all there ahead of me and Bokko and Bertha.

I had so many questions to ask Miss Agnes. Why'd she come back to us? Why didn't she go back to England? And most of all, how long would she stay?

But when I saw her standing by the big map on the wall, I felt so stuffed up with crying and laughing I couldn't say anything. I just stared and stared, trying to make it feel real that she was standing there, just like last year.

Miss Agnes turned to smile at us when we came in and then she raised her eyebrow, that way she has. "Fred," she said, "I never saw you so quiet."

I just held the tea pot out to her.

"I don't need it to remember you by any more," I said.

Chapter 2

Bertha and Bokko and me sat down in our old desks. Miss Agnes already had new name cards taped on them. My name is really Frederika, but the only place I ever saw it written was on the name card on my desk. Because everyone calls me just Fred.

Miss Agnes' desk was in the corner just like last year and the big table in the middle just like last year, and our desks all around in a circle sort of. Just like last year.

All the kids looked different, a little, even it was only a few months since I saw them last. Especially Little Pete. He's the tallest person in our village even he's not grown yet. He even has to bend his head a little to come in the door. And he got even bigger since last spring I could see, because his pants were way up by the top of his boots.

And Selena and Charlie-Boy had lost a lot of teeth.

All us kids just watched Miss Agnes.

She looked the same, only different. Her hair was shorter but it still flew around some kind of way. Like it was made of cobwebs. And she was still skinny. And there were the pants.

She moved fast, like she always did, handing out pencils and things, acting like there was nothing special about that day.

I could see everyone was feeling like me. Kind of crazy-happy. We were so glad to be back in our school with things from last year on the walls and her right there, and the wood stove crackling. Charlie-Boy was getting ready to be really silly I could tell because he was jittering up and down in his seat. But he's only seven.

I'll bet Miss Agnes was afraid to look at us too much because we were all so half-wild. Like a gone-to-seed dandelion, if you puff on it, like she'd say something and we'd all blow into the air.

But she knew we wanted to know why she'd changed her mind. Why she came back. So finally she stopped buzzing around and she folded her arms across her middle like she always did and she said, " Okay. You tell me about your summer and I'll tell you about mine." Then she suddenly unfolded her arms again and walked across the room.

But I'm forgetting," she said. "Fred and Bokko have to meet our cat."

Miss Agnes opened the door to the little book room and made a chirrup sound. The cat came out, blinking like he'd been asleep. He put out his two front paws and stretched out, like dogs do when they want to play. Then he yawned and Bokko and I pulled in our breath when we saw his sharp white teeth and his pink tongue.

Before Miss Agnes, none of us kids had ever seen a cat. Just in books. He didn't look so yellow like he did last night by the lamp, he was more orange, with eyes the same color, and stripes on his tail. We were all a little afraid of him, but the cat wasn't afraid of us. He jumped up on Bokko's desk and rolled onto his back, stretching out his two front paws to her face. Bokko's eyes were just big and she looked scared.

"He wants you to pet him," said Miss Agnes. Miss Agnes put her hand down and the cat rubbed his head against her stiff fingers, up and down, eyes closed.

"He's petting his *self*," said Selina.

Bokko slowly petted the cat with one finger under his ear, and when he turned over to stretch out on his belly, she smoothed all the white fur on the cat's front legs. Bokko gave me her special look that means that something is wonderful.

We were so quiet watching the cat, we could hear the deep sound he made in his chest.

"That's purring. It means he's happy," Miss Agnes said. Miss Agnes took Bokko's hand and put it easy on the cat's back so Bokko could feel the purring, even she couldn't hear it. You should have seen the look on Bokko's face when she felt that sound.

"We had a dog that color once," Roger said .

"In England he'd be called a ginger tom. That's what we call that color. Ginger. And tom is what we call a male cat. So he's a ginger tom," Miss Agnes said.

"How old is he?" I asked.

"He's very young, still growing," Miss Agnes said.

"Will he have babies?" asked Selina. Miss Agnes raised both eyebrows and shook her head. Everyone laughed because there are no other cats anywhere on the Kokyukuk. And besides, he was a boy.

But Selina's only seven, like Charlie Boy.

Miss Agnes showed us the sign for cat, fingers and thumbs together to make whiskers on the side of the nose. You could do it with one hand or both. All the signs for animals are so easy to remember because they sort of draw the animal.

Miss Agnes has been teaching Bokko sign language but all of us are learning it too. Even people in town, even the old men who sit around the store, they know how to say hi and a few other things. But us kids are the best at it.

Of course we all used to talk to Bokko with our hands before. Like we'd point where we were going, or show with our hands what we were going to do, like Mama would pretend kneading with her hand and point, to tell Bokko to get the big bread pan so they could start making bread. But we couldn't say the words about feelings, like pretty and dirty and being mad and all that. So those were the signs we liked the most.

It's easy, sign language, but Miss Agnes doesn't think so because she forgets the signs sometimes. She really frowns when that happens. She says it's because she has an old brain. She says that's why we have to learn everything we can when we're young. Because it gets harder to learn when you get old.

"Cat name?" Bokko signed.

"I just call him Puss." Miss Agnes spelled that out for her with the sign alphabet. " My mother called all her cats Puss," she said.

We were all quiet, and then Charlie-Boy frowned down at his desk and said, "That's a sissy name."

Miss Agnes made her wouldn't-you-know-it face and laughed. "Well, you think of a good name for him. Or better still, wait for a name to happen. Sometimes names just happen."

MIss Agnes folded her arms around herself again and looked at us. "Now we're ready for the questions," she said.

I was scared all of a sudden. What if it wasn't true? What if she wasn't going to stay? What if she was just here for a week or something? Maybe everyone felt like that because no one asked anything for a minute. Finally Roger did.

"Did you go to England?" he asked.

"Yes. I went to New York in the train, and then I flew across the ocean in a big plane."

She looked at Roger and said in a show-offy kind of way, "A Lockheed Constellation." Because Roger was crazy about airplanes. I think he knew about every one that was.

"Whoa," said Roger. " A Lockheed Constellation," like she'd said she'd been flying on a magic carpet or something. Miss Agnes smiled at him. "I knew you'd be impressed with that. I brought you a picture of it. I'll show you later," she said.

Then she showed us on the big map where she'd traveled. It's as big as the whole wall, that map. Even Miss Agnes has to stand on a chair to touch Alaska way up at the top.

She went from our village to Fairbanks with Sam, and then to Anchorage on the train, and then on a plane to Seattle, and then the train to New York, and then across the ocean to London. And then she took a train to her own town. Cambridge.

We could hardly imagine such a long trip. "About eight thousand miles," she said. "Four thousand there, four thousand back."

We were all quiet a minute, trying to think how far that was.

"And I used to think it was a long way to Fairbanks," said Kenny.

"That Kings' Choir?" I asked. "Did you hear them?" She used to play that record for us last year. That choir lives in her town. They sing in a big church that's made of rock and so the sound is really loud. There's a picture of that church on front of the record cover.

She smiled and nodded. "They were as wonderful as I remembered," she said.

"And those pink trees?" I asked.

"Oh, yes, but they only bloom in the spring, you know. So they weren't pink like the ones in the pictures I showed you last year."

"And did you go on the train that goes underground?" said Plasker.

"Yes," she said. "I have a picture of that, too."

She reached up to the shelf over the wash basin to get the big box of pictures she kept there. I think she had pictures of everything you could think of. Some were pictures she took herself with her camera and some were pictures she cut out of books and stuff. We were so happy she'd brought that box back with her. It was one of our best things.

When the bombs were dropping on England the people had to get into safe places that were underground. Like the tube. The tube was what that underground train was called because it's a big place with a curved ceiling. She said it was like being inside a gigantic pipe. And all the people used to sleep down there in the war when the enemies were bombing them. Because the bombs couldn't reach down there. In the picture there was about a mile of people all jammed together, lying down.

"More people that live on our whole Koyukuk River," said Jimmy. Bokko was thinking that too, because she made the sign for lots, with her eyes big.

Miss Agnes laughed. "More people than live in all of Alaska almost," she said.

"I'd like to live in a place like that," said Toby Joe.

Miss Agnes looked at him. "I wonder if you would," she said. "When you live in a little place like this everyone is important. Everyone is interested in everything you do, and they know everything you ever did."

"Yeah and then they tell my mom on me," said Plasker, and we all laughed because Plasker is always getting in some kind of trouble.

"People are not so interested in each other when there are lots of them, like in London," said Miss Agnes. "I'd forgotten that a lot of people keep themselves to themselves in England. People on the street don't often talk to each other. Often they don't look at each other when they're passing by in a crowd. I was so used to life in the villages I think I startled some

14

people, greeting them even though they were strangers." Miss Agnes laughed a little, thinking about how she had been when she first got back to England.

It was a very funny thing to think about, people so stuck up. Keeping themselves to themselves, like Miss Agnes said.

"And here people help each other," Miss Agnes said.

We were all quiet, thinking about that. "Like if someone is sick," said Toby Joe.

"Or if they need something, like they're running out of wood," said Marie. "Or maybe when they're just sad, because of something, like when Roger's brother died, then everyone goes to sit with them."

"That's what I mean," said Miss Agnes.

I was thinking that another thing about not having very many people is that you haven't got so many to fight with. Even when you get mad at someone here you don't stay mad for a long time. You have to make up with that person and find someone else to be mad at. Like when Julia and Martha have a fight they're yelling at each other in the store and the next day they're all happy again and they're mad at Sally instead. Because there aren't enough people to stay mad or if you did pretty soon you'd be mad at everyone. So you kind of have to trade off.

"Were you happy to be home in England?" asked Bertha.

"Yes," Miss Agnes said. "But it's very different there now. For one thing there are whole blocks in London still full of rubble from the bombing. You remember we talked about that?"

"The blitzkreig," said Jimmy. He *always* remembered the hard names for things.

"What's rubble?" asked Plasker.

"That's all the bricks and timber the buildings were made of that the bombs knocked down into the street," she said. She frowned at the map for a minute as if she could still see the mess.

"And the food has to be rationed," she said. She told us about the little ticket books you needed for getting some things like sugar and butter. No one could buy too much, it had to be spread around so that everyone got some. Otherwise greedy people might buy everything and leave nothing for the others. It surprised us to think that anyone would do that. In the Indian way we share everything. Like when a hunter gets a caribou, then the hunter gets the littlest meat. Not the most.

I think she wanted that to be enough so she said, "When I was finished seeing things I came back." We were all looking at her so hard that she cleared her throat.

"Was that why you came back, because of the little books?" asked Bertha.

Miss Agnes laughed. "No," she said.

"Why then?" said Bertha.

Miss Agnes turned to the blackboard and lined up the chalk in a row. Then she turned around again. "I have *no* idea," she said and she made her funny face. Miss Agnes would always make a joke if she didn't want to answer something. Like when we asked her if she ever had a boyfriend. Or when we asked her how old she was. But we wanted so much to know why she came back we kept after her.

So finally she said, " I had to show you this cat, didn't I? You've never seen a cat, so when I got him I said, I have to go back to show them this cat!"

We knew Miss Agnes didn't really come back because of the cat.

But maybe it was a *little* because of the cat. She always wanted us to know everything we didn't know.

But we were all afraid to ask her how long she'd stay this time.

Chapter 3

Miss Agnes gave us back the dictionaries we'd had last year. They weren't real dictionaries. Just some little noteooks where Miss Agnes wrote the words we asked for when we were writing our stories. With a separate page for each letter. Like she'd write "beautiful" on the b page. And then the next time we needed that word it would be in the book and we wouldn't have to ask her again.

I wonder what it would be like to have all the words in the world stuffed into your head, like Miss Agnes.

Seeing those dictionaries made us wild to write and we asked her if we could do that first. She smiled and then she went into the book room and brought out a box filled with black and white books. They had lines on the pages and they were just for writing stories in. Last year we just had some paper stapled together for our stories, so we were happy to have these new notebooks.

When Miss Agnes first came we didn't know anything about writing stories, and we said we couldn't do it, but she made us write a story every day, even the little ones who couldn't spell. They'd tell her what their story was and she'd write it down and then they had to copy it. She said writing was something you had to do every day, too, like reading. No use just once in awhile.

At first we didn't think we had anything to write about but after awhile we found out that we had everything to write about. We got so used to it that we wanted to do it every day, first thing.

And we'd read the stories out loud, and we'd draw pictures to go with the stories, and everything.

All summer I thought of things I wanted to write about, but there wasn't any extra paper at fish camp, and most of the time no one could even find the pencil we used to write down the number of fish each day. So I was stuffed up with stories from all summer.

I could see everyone else felt like that, too, because they all had their heads down, just quiet, writing away.

Before I started, though, I wrote down what Bokko signed to me for her story. About her and Marie washing the clothes in the old gas washer and it ran out of gas and they had to wash all those clothes by hand with the horrible old scrub board. Bokko knew how to write some of the words but not a lot of them, because she just came to school for the first time last year, when Miss Agnes came. Our other teachers wouldn't teach her, because she was deaf. So Bokko had a lot of catching up to do.

Miss Agnes put a strip of masking tape on little Benny's desk under his name card and she wrote the alphabet on that strip.

"Now you're going to learn to write," she said.

Benny was left-handed so Miss Agnes showed him how to turn his paper so the corner was pointing at his stomach. That way he didn't have to twist his hand. We were really interested in that.

"Big Bernie, my auntie, is left handed," Little Pete told her. "She said when she went to the mission school the teachers used to hit her left hand with a ruler if she used it. She still has a big lump on her hand even. And she writes all sideways with her hand scrunched up."

Miss Agnes frowned her worst frown when Pete told her that. She told us how silly it was to care which hand someone writes with. As if there was something wrong with being left handed.

Little Benny was looking at us in a worried way. So Miss Agnes said, "Besides, left-handed people are *always* very smart." Benny really looked happy when she said that.

Once while we were writing Miss Agnes looked up suddenly and raised her eyebrow at Roger, "Neat, remember." She said that because last year Roger wrote really sloppy most of the time and Miss Agnes said there was no sense writing something if no one could read it.

"Neat," said Roger, and he made a salute at Miss Agnes.

We read our stories out loud when we were finished and we looked at everyone's pictures they made for the story. Little Benny stood up and told us what he'd had Miss Agnes write in his book.

" I come to school now." And he had made a picture of him with a big head and big eyes and stick legs. Like his really were. His eyes were so round and proud when he told us what his story said that my throat got that tight feeling. I wish me and Bokko had a little brother like him.

Jimmy wrote a funny story about how he didn't have anything to read in the summer after he came back from fish camp so he read Old Man Andreson's medical book, all of it. And it's really, really fat, that book. ButJimmy said the worst thing was that every time he read about a new disease he started to think he had it. Like this one disease you get from eating meat that isn't cooked enough and you get worms in your muscles. Jimmy wrote that he could really feel them in his muscles for awhile. We really laughed about that.

Before it was time for lunch, the *Idler* came. That's the sternwheeler George Black brings up the Koyukuk every year. It's got a big paddle wheel. It was pushing one barge and it was really loaded with stuff, all the stuff Old Man Andreson gets for the store in the winter.

When George blew the whistle on the boat we all jumped to our feet. We knew Miss Agnes would let us run down to the slip and see what came. Miss Agnes looked as excited as we were.

"Oh good," she said. "I'm glad it came during school. I need all of you to help carry up the things for the school."

"Did you get lots of things for our school, Miss Agnes?" I asked.

"Oh, yes," she said, just happy. "Oh my, yes."

Everyone from town was down at the slip before we got there.

The gangplank was out and all the men and boys were stacking the boxes and crates in the big cart that George kept on the deck to unload the boat with. They were all laughing and calling out the names of the things in the boxes.

"I see you got my sardines," Gilbert Derendorff yelled to Old Man Andreson. We all laughed because I think that's all Gilbert ever eats.

They made a pile of boxes for the store, all the pilot bread cases and macaroni and flour and sugar and powdered milk and dried eggs and slabs of bacon and canned peaches and rice and canned milk, and about a thousand gunnysacks of beans and all the other stuff we need every year. And they put the barrel of coal oil we use for our lamps and the boxes of gas in another place and then they started making a smaller pile of things for the school.

Everyone stopped to look at this big bunch of geese flying over us because they were flying really really low, lower than we ever saw them. They were flying so low you could even see the patterns on their chests and their white cheeks. And they were making a big racket, noisy as all get out.

We all laughed and laughed. It was just like those geese were trying to see what came on the barge, too. And then having a big argument about it. I thought that would be a good story to write for the next day.

I knew everyone was thinking that those geese meant winter would be coming soon because they were going south for the winter. It's kind of a lonesome feeling when the birds fly away, really. There's hardly any birds left after it snows.

Bertha and me carried two boxes up to the school, really heavy ones. We were just puffing. We wanted to help Miss Agnes open them so we could see what was in them, but she just shooshed us away with her hand. "Go get the rest of them," she said, so we hurried back down to the slip to get more.

We passed Bokko and Marie carrying a great big box between them. They're really strong, those two. Bertha signed "tough" to them and they laughed.

After people packed all the things into the store they began to bring the school stuff up. Barney Sam and Clayton Malemute brought the big heavy boxes in the cart and Gilbert carried one on his back with a tump line. I think they were as interested as we were to see what was in them.

Especially Barney Sam. He went to school with Miss Agnes up at Allakaket a long time ago, so he was always interested in our school and what we did. Boys only go to school in between fall and marten trapping and beaver trapping and spring camp, so it's hard for them that way. Even the ones who like school, when they get to be big boys they stop going at all because then they have to do a man's work at home. But Barney missed school, he said.

When we had all the boxes in the school we started to open them, even Barney and Clayton and Gilbert. There were boxes of paper to draw on and paint on, and writing paper and new boxes of paints and crayons like she brought last year, and a lot more records. And lots of notebooks, little ones and big ones and a whole box of folders in all different colors. I hoped I'd get a red one.

The ginger tom kept getting in the boxes and hiding. And when we reached in for something he'd jump up and slap at our hands with his paws. You could tell he thought it was very funny to scare us.

And there were boxes and boxes and boxes of books.

I wanted to see Jimmy's face when he saw the books Miss Agnes had brought. Jimmy liked to read more than anyone in the world. And Miss Agnes had brought eight big boxes of books for us.

But Jimmy and Kenny were still down at the *Idler,* looking at George's new inboard engine. Jimmy was as interested in machinery things as he was in everything else, and Kenny was almost the same. Sometimes Old Man Andreson had Jimmy come to help him fix his little generator. So they wouldn't be back in school for awhile.

Miss Agnes wouldn't care if they were late. She said you learn as much out of school as you do in it.

We could hardly believe those books. We never saw so many. We stacked them under the windows because we didn't have enough shelves to put them in. But Miss Agnes said we'd make more shelves out of gas boxes.

The books weren't new. Miss Agnes said she'd gotten them for nothing from this place and that, but that we were all such good readers now that she needed a lot more books for us. There were books for the little kids and fat ones for the big kids and every other kind of books you could think of.

And one box had nothing but these yellow magazines. National Geographics. They were used too, but they were really shiny and smelled good, like I don't know what.

We almost stopped work then because nothing was so interesting as those magazines. We wanted to sit down and read those National Geographics right away. Or at least look at the pictures because they had some hard writing. That kind with little letters, crammed up.

It was like it always was with Miss Agnes. Everything new and exciting.

And there was one big, heavy box which Miss Agnes wouldn't let us open. She had Little Pete put it back in the book room.

"It's a surprise," she said.

After school Bertha and me went to the store to see all the new groceries. There was a case of canned pineapple, that we never saw before. I knew Mamma wouldn't buy any because she doesn't like to try new things.

Then Old Man Andreson showed us some pretty little boxes with white and blue and red paper wrappers.

"These here are marshmallows," he said. He opened a box for us and it was full of white things shaped like little cans. Ten of them, all lined up in the box.

"What are they for, Jack?" I asked. "Beats me," he said. "I just know the visiting nurse asked if I had some last time she was here. She said she put them to melt in her cocoa."

He gave us each one to try. We tried taking little bites off the sides but Old Man Andreson popped one into his mouth whole. "Like this," he said.

That marshmallow felt so funny in my mouth, all squishy. Not like anything else we ever ate. But it was delicious. When we finished he laughed because we had white sugar powder on our lips.

"Some new kind of candy, I guess," Bertha said.

I wished we could eat the whole box. Another thing Mamma wouldn't ever buy for sure.

Mamma was there helping Old Man Andreson, like she did lots of times. She told us to clean off the last shelves that were still empty. So we did that with Mamma's rags and the bucket of soapy water. And then Bertha and me opened the last boxes.

There was a case of soap to wash clothes with. Rinso White it's called. There's a song on the radio about that soap every day nearly, and we all know it, so Bertha and I started singing it, "happy little Rinso, happy little Rinso," to make old Man Andreson laugh.

But it's kind of a dumb song.

We just loved it when the store was full up of groceries and stuff in the fall. It felt like we were rich.

Chapter 4

Before Miss Agnes came, going to school in September was hard. Seems like the sun is always shining bright in September, not like August when sometimes it rains all the time. And the leaves are so beautiful then, lemon and lime, like it says on our crayons. And all the gnats and mosquitoes are gone. Everybody around here always says it's the best time of year.

Even though I liked school, it was hard to be indoors in September. But when Miss Agnes came to teach us we hardly noticed that it was so nice out-doors because it was so interesting indoors.

Miss Agnes had Jimmy and Roger bring up all the gas boxes she'd talked Old Man Andreson out of and the next day we painted them all different colors and the day after that we put the books away.

These gas boxes are the ones they ship gas in for our boats and for old man Andreson's little generator. There are two big square tin cans in each gas box. They hold five gallons in each one. We use those cans for everything.

Last year Miss Agnes had us see how many quarts of water would go in those cans when we were learning about measuring and stuff, and we weighed them to see how much water weighed. A lot! It's more than eight pounds for a gallon. I can carry two five gallon cans of water from the river, half filled up, one in each hand, and that's about forty pounds, so I'm strong for my age.

But you have to wrap something around the wire handles or those handles will cut your hands off, nearly. You have to wash those cans out with soap and water real good before you use them for water or anything. Then you can cut the top off to carry water or cut down the sides to use it for a dishpan or a pan to feed dogs or anything you can think of but you got to be careful to roll the edges over with pliers so no one would cut themselves on them.

And then the wooden boxes the gas comes in can be used for anything you want, too. Because they're really strong. Like you stand it on end and it's a good chair, and everyone uses them sideways for shelves. No one ever threw a gas can or a gas box away, I'll bet.

Bertha wanted to put the books in the shelves by size but Miss Agnes said we had to put them by the alphabet, which I thought was a very good idea. Like if you had a book by someone whose name started with an A that book would go right on the first shelf. So you could find them easier. But then I remembered that you'd have to know who wrote the books you were looking for. I don't actually know the name of anyone who wrote a book.

Then there was one shelf just for science books, and different kinds of books that weren't stories.

She didn't want us to put the little kids' books by themself because she said anyone could read those books. We shouldn't say books were for little kids or big kids because everyone can like every kind of book. It doesn't matter, if it's good. So the books were all mixed up.

And Miss Agnes said anyone in town could come to borrow our books.

"You mean to take home?" Plasker said. When she nodded we were so surprised. Our other teachers wouldn't let even us kids take books home. I thought right then that I'd take Grandpa some of those yellow magazines. National Geographics. I could hardly wait to see his face.

"Did you read this summer?" she asked, looking at us as if she didn't think we had.

"Oh, I read a lot," I said. "My uncle at fish camp, he has a lot of books and I read them all about six times. About cowboys and stuff. Louis L'Amour."

"Oh yes," said Miss Agnes in a funny way. "Louis L'Amour. Very popular in Allakaket, too."

I was very pleased that Miss Agnes knew about those books.

"Have you read them too?"

"No," said Miss Agnes. "Do you think I should read them?"

"Oh yes," I said. " They're really, really good."

Everybody else told what they'd read in the summer, but no one read as much as me. That's because hardly nobody has books at home or in the fish camp like my uncle.

I told that to Miss Agnes and she said next year we should all take books with us when we go to camp.

That would be really good.

Every day someone came to see our cat, and we'd tell them what ginger tom meant. But a name didn't really happen to him, the way Miss Agnes thought it might. We mostly just called him ginger tom. No one called him Puss, except Miss Agnes.

Miss Agnes said that was okay because cats didn't care a fig about their names. Not like dogs. Whatever a fig is.

Gilbert and Bertha's mom and Clayton and them came to see him, and Kenny's mom and dad, and a bunch of others.

And Grandpa and all of grandpa's old friends came, the ones that drink tea at Grandpa's house every day. Of course they wait til after Grandma's done her work because she says she doesn't like to have men under her feet.

They don't have so much to do like when they were younger, and some of them can't get around too good anymore. So they spend a lot of time with Grandpa.

Even if they're a little scared of Grandma because she just talks right out and says what she thinks.

And Miss Toby came to school too. She's really really old, and can only speak Indian. But Marie can tell us what she says. That's because Marie's Mamma talks Indian to her. Mamma never does, just to Grandma and Grandpa. So I don't know much Indian, just the short words.

Miss Toby was the best one to tell us things about the old days. Like how her mamma had a tattoo on her chin because she was raised way down river where they did that. And how everyone back then used bows and arrows even if they had guns, because the shells cost too much. And were hard to get. Even grandpa said he used bows and arrows when he was little. Sometimes Grandpa would make a little bow for Roger's little brothers and them, just to show them.

Miss Toby told us how you say cat in Athabascan. *Gusge.* Miss Agnes said that's the Russian word for cat, too. She told us the Indians took lots of words from the Russians for things they didn't have. Like tea and sugar in Athabascan, *tsaaye* and *saahele.* Those are really Russian words.

Lots of the old people had seen cats before. In the old days when the miners were here there were lots of cats, they said. Like little lynx said Grandpa. No tufts on the ears, though. Our cat was very friendly, and rubbed against them and they liked that.

Grandpa's friend, Luke Simon, really liked our cat and he came to see him lots. Our cat would jump on his lap and knead. Just like Mamma kneading bread! The first time he did that we laughed so hard. Miss Agnes said that's how baby kittens start their mother's milk and so he did it whenever he was feeling really comfortable. Even though he wasn't a baby.

Luke told us about an old miner who lived on the Yukon when he was a little boy. That man had a cat and a dog and a weasel and a marten and a porcupine and a squirrel and they all lived together in one house and never fought. And a ptarmigan he raised from a baby, too. I would like more than anything to see them all together like that.

Selina liked that story so well she made a picture of all those animals sitting together. Selina is really, really good at drawing.

Last year we'd learned all the names of all the countries and the continents on our big map. Miss Agnes said this year we would learn the names of the big cities and the rivers and all the names of the states in America. But we never say someone is going to America. We say they're going *outside*. That's what we call all those states. Outside.

When we'd only been in school a few days Miss Agnes brought out a little box with pins in it that we were going to use to mark places on the map. Every little pin had a colored ball on the top. They were so pretty. I wished I could play with them.

Miss Agnes showed us on the map where Bokko's school was, the deaf school she'd go to when she was fourteen. To learn how to sign real good. Miss Agnes put a pin with a red ball on that spot. Oregon.

When Miss Agnes began talking to Mamma last year about that school for Bokko Mamma was mad. Even Grandpa, who really liked school and was so happy that Bokko was learning. He didn't want Bokko to go away.

A lot of people around here were taken to the mission schools when they were little. And they didn't like it much. Too strict and they got smacked for

35

speaking Indian, and lots of other things. And they never came home for years and years because the mission teachers didn't want them to be around people who spoke Indian. So some of them even forgot how. That's how come no one's too happy about people going out to school.

But Miss Agnes talked and talked about how Bokko could learn more out there because this school was just for deaf children. She said it would be good for Bokko to be around other deaf children. She said when you're the only one it makes you feel different, and so it was good to know there were lots of other people just like you.

Miss Agnes said teaching deaf children was very special and you needed a lot of training to do it. And she didn't have that training so she couldn't do a very good job for Bokko. Like we can only tell Bokko some of the stuff that we're talking about in school because we don't know enough signs.

And maybe Bokko could learn to read lips too, and that would help her a lot. And how to talk even. And Bokko could come home in the summer, and she wouldn't have to stay away for years, like they used to at the mission schools. Just long enough to learn to get along in her reading and writing and that so she could talk to people who couldn't do signs.

And so Mamma and Grandpa said Bokko could go.

Grandma was still mad, though.

Miss Agnes went to Bokko's school before she came back to us. She talked to the teachers and them, and they gave her a list of the most important words for Bokko to learn to sign before she came. And they gave Miss Agnes a little book about the school. She showed it to us. There were a lot of smiling people in the pictures and all the children slept in a big room with a lot of beds. When she finished showing us the pictures she gave Bokko the book to keep. You should have seen Bokko's face. She was scared and happy at the same time.

Me too, because I'm scared to think about Bokko going away outside to school. All by herself, no Mamma, no Grandpa, no Grandma. And no Marie. That's Bokko's best friend. And no me.

But I'm happy, too.

I don't like it when you have two different feelings about something.

And then Miss Agnes really surprised us. She put another pin in the map pretty close to Bokko's pin. A green one.

"That's Washington," she said. "There's a school there for boys like Jimmy, to get them ready for college. I told them about Jimmy and they said If Jimmy can pass the test in the spring he can go there next year."

"Whoa," said Roger. That was his favorite word for surprises. We all looked at Jimmy. We could tell that Miss Agnes had told him all about it before, because of his smile.

Jimmy was the smartest one in the school. Maybe in the whole world. He could think of questions about anything, stuff you'd never even think about, like snow and stars and rocks. But before Miss Agnes came he didn't have anyone to ask, except about engines and things.

He's interested in everything, really, whatever anyone is doing. Like he even asks us kids questions about how we made something, or why we liked a certain book. Like when Miss Agnes gave Roger the picture of that big airplane Jimmy asked Roger all about it, why it had three tails and all.

There's nothing Jimmy isn't curious about, that's what Grandpa says. Because Jimmy always wants Grandpa to show him how to do stuff. And Grandpa says when Jimmy was little like Charlie-Boy he drove everyone crazy with his questions.

Jimmy has this way of looking at you, really serious, when he wants to know something. He sort of makes you feel important, that you can tell him something he wants to know. And when he's doing something, like reading, or working on his papers, he has this other look. Like he's deep, deep down in himself.

He really likes science the most. Last year Miss Agnes got a microscope for us, and Jimmy hardly did anything else but look at things with it. Just looking down into that eye thing, pushing away his hair that always falls down in his face. And then Miss Agnes told him there were microscopes that could show a lot, lot more than our one.

Then she read us this story about this boy named Michael Farraday, who was just this ordinary boy long ago, really poor, too, and he got to be the most important scientist. He found out about electricity. And he was just from a little village like us, and his father was a blacksmith. That's a person who makes horseshoes and that. So that's how Jimmy got to wanting to be a scientist.

And now he was going to go to a special school to get ready for college. And get to be a scientist. Just like Miss Agnes told us. We could do anything we wanted, even if we were from a tiny village far away from anything.

"What did your dad say?" Roger asked in a worried way. I wanted to know too, because Jimmy's dad is kind of ornery. That's what Grandpa says about him.

Jimmy made a funny face. "He told Miss Agnes, who's going to pay for *that*? And Miss Agnes told him I'd have a scholarship." We all looked at Miss Agnes to see what that meant.

39

"It means it's free," she said. So that was a good thing.

"So he just walked away when she said that. 'Long as I don't have to pay,' he said."

Even if Jimmy was smart, I felt worried about the test. We never did tests, not the kind with paper.

"Is the test hard," Miss Agnes?" I said.

"Very hard," she said. "There are six parts." She told us he'd have to know science and English and stuff like books and music and art, and Arithmetic. Miss Agnes calls that mathematics. And history and geography. And there's a writing test.

"There's not much time to learn all this. Jimmy will have to study and study," she said.

Well, we knew he could do *that*, because he always studied.

But I knew by everyone's faces that the idea of the test was going to worry us all.

Chapter 5

Bokko was learning a lot of new signs from her signing book, and us too because we'd practice them with her. Like if she learned to sign the word fancy, we'd all practice it too, and then we'd try to use it every day for awhile until it was stuck in our mind. It was really funny because we'd all sign the new word for crazy things, like Jimmy signed "fancy" when Little Pete broke his shoe lace and tied the ends together in a lumpy knot.

Charlie-Boy was the best at signing out of all of us. He never forgot any signs. And he learned them without even hardly practicing. So Bokko would look at him if she didn't understand something, like what everyone was laughing about, and he'd try to sign it for her. And Miss Agnes would ask Charlie for the sign she needed if she couldn't remember it. Miss Agnes called Charlie-Boy "our dictionary."

Miss Agnes is very, very picky about writing. The little ones had to practice their printing every day because it isn't easy to do it the way Miss Agnes wants it. Like Charlie-Boy always had to write a lot of k's. Ks are hard because the little one and the big one are almost the same but not quite. So you have to be careful.

If us big ones wrote something sloppy she'd make us do it over.

She taught Bertha how to write cursive last year because Bertha's printing was so good. She wouldn't let the rest of us do it until ours was that good. But when she came back she said all the rest of us except the little ones were going to start learning cursive. We were really happy. I like the way things are all curvy with cursive.

She said she didn't care if we wrote things in cursive, she just cared if we could read it because lots of people wrote in cursive. And the best way to learn to read cursive was to write it. But I will write everything in cursive when I learn because I like the way it looks.

Everybody had different arithmetic papers because we were all in different places. Like Benny had a paper with counting on it and he had to write the number really careful in the box. "Straight back, fat belly, hat," he'd say like how Miss Agnes taught him to write a five. She had a sort of story for every number so the little kids could remember how it looked when they were first learning.

"It's really hard to write a five," she told him. Miss Agnes always said something was hard. All our other teachers used to tell us things were easy. And then we'd feel bad if we had a hard time learning it. When Miss Agnes said it was hard it *would* be hard at first like she said but we wouldn't feel bad because she told us it would be. Hard. And then it would get easy and we'd feel really proud because we'd learned another hard thing.

When we finished learning one kind of math, like adding two numbers, then we'd go to the next thing. But some of us took a long time on some things. I was learning long division and I think I was going to be doing it for a long, long time. Miss Agnes said it didn't matter if you were slow or fast at learning something new because in the end you'd know it just the same whether you'd been fast or slow.

That was good because arithmetic was not a thing I was fast at.

When I started those hard multiplications last year Miss Agnes taught me to turn the paper sideways. That way you always have lines to keep your numbers straight. Because if you go crooked you will get everything all wrong. And you do that with long division too, turn your paper sideways. Miss Agnes knows a lot of ways to make things easier.

The first time Miss Agnes brought out her little concertina we sang all the old songs we learned last year, really loud. The old miners used to call a concertina a squeeze box, Grandpa said, because you push it in and out while you play on the keys. I tried it once and it is not even a little bit easy to do that.

Our ginger tom didn't like the concertina and ran back into the book room and didn't come out until we were finished. Maybe he wouldn't have minded if we weren't singing so loud, but we were so happy to have our songs back again that we couldn't help it.

Then Miss Agnes asked us to sing her some new ones. She meant the ones we learned off the radio that summer. So we taught her one we really, really liked. "Sixteen Tons." The boys sang that one crazy loud. "Some people think a man is made out of mud!"

And we taught her "So Long It's Been Good to Know You." That one is good, too, but I was glad we didn't learn it before Miss Agnes got back or maybe it would have made us think about her all the time.

Miss Agnes always liked to learn new songs, even though I think she knew a million already. When she played at our dances the old people would ask her for something they remembered from long ago that they learned from the old miners and them, before there was radio. Like "Annie Laurie" and "Bicycle Built for Two" and "Red River Valley." And Grandpa and them would just be singing away with her concertina.

Miss Agnes always knows the songs the old people ask for. She says that's because you never forget songs. She says all the songs I know now I will know when I am ninety-seven.

I wonder if that is true.

Chapter 6

I stayed after school lots to help Miss Agnes. I liked to do that because after school Miss Agnes plays records, lots of different ones she hasn't played for us. Like she played this opera one for me about a poor girl who is dying. She has t.b. just like my dad had. That song feels so sad, even you don't know what the words mean.

And she always has tea when she works after school and I have some too.

I'd clean the coal oil lamps or wipe off the desks and sweep, and stuff like that. I had to dust more than last year, too, because our ginger tom sheds something awful and his fur gets all over.

Little Pete's the one who mostly splits the school's wood and makes the kindling, and he brings the water from the river, too. But usually I'm the one cleans the ashes out of the stove and brings in wood from the wood pile for the next day. Little Pete says I'm as good as any boy for hard work. That's Little Pete. He always says these nice things that make you feel good.

And sometimes Jimmy stayed after school too, so Miss Agnes could help him with something. But Jimmy would be sort of jumpy, afraid his dad would be mad if he was late home.

Jimmy really had a lot of studying to do, but he tried not to take too much home. Jimmy said it made his dad grouchy to see those books. And because Jimmy's brother Paddy would want to do Jimmy's chores so Jimmy could study.

Paddy was really a nice guy. He went to school for awhile when I was just little like Benny but his dad made him stay home when he got big. I wondered if Paddy missed school like Barney did.

Jimmy and Paddy had a lot of work to do at home because they didn't have a mother. She died when they had so much measles here one time. Little Pete's mother too, she died from the measles that same time. A lot of people did.

So Jimmy did the cooking and he even knew how to make bread. He asked Grandma and she showed him. Jimmy said his bread wasn't very good, but still.

Even they had so much to do at home, hauling water and cooking and that, and setting snares for rabbit, and hunting, Jimmy and Paddy still helped people. Like they always split wood for Grandpa. They were really fast at that. I liked to watch them, just zinging away with the axe, wood just flying.

Grandma and Grandpa really like Paddy and Jimmy. And they help them, too. Like Grandma always knits them socks and hats and gloves and stuff. And Grandma grabs Jimmy every time she can to give him a haircut because his hair is always too long and hanging in his face. Grandma said Paddy and Jimmy were just like their mother, who was a really good woman. That's what Grandma says. Always helping people, too. Grandma says their mother would be just proud of how her big boys turned out.

I wonder if they think about her a lot, like I think about our dad.

Every day when we came to school our ginger tom was waiting for us. He sat on the long table in the middle of the room and everyone who came in he'd hump his back up and give a little mew. We said he was very polite and that mew meant hello. And the back meant don't forget to pet me. And it looked like he could count because if someone was missing he'd jump up on the window sill and look out as if he was waiting.

Like when the boys went out chicken hunting in the morning. You can get lots of them in the fall with a .22. That's what we call spruce hens. Chickens.

We have different names for lots of things. Like we call the engines on our boats kickers. Miss Agnes says she likes that word, kicker. Because that's what the little propeller does, kick the water sort of.

Anyway, the boys, Little Pete and Jimmy and Roger and Kenny and Plasker, brought chickens to everyone in the village who didn't hunt, like Old Miss Toby, and Grandpa and Mamma and like that. It was sort of like their job because in the Indian way young people must take care of the older ones.

So they'd be a little bit late and our cat would look for them.

Our old teachers used to get mad about them being late, but Miss Agnes said hunting was as important as school.

We wondered what our cat would think when some of the kids went out to the trapline at marten season and didn't come to school at all for awhile.

After school I went to Old Man Andreson's store to see if Mamma was there and to see if the shelves Bertha and I set up were still neat like we left them. Mamma was already gone. There wasn't hardly anyone in the store because fall was always a busy time. Because of hunting, and cutting wood, and getting the last fish. Getting ready for winter.

While I was there Sam White flew over the store and made a loud noise with his engine. He always said he did that to wake up Old Man Andreson.

Old Man Andreson left me to take care of the store while he went to the landing strip with the big wheel barrow to help Sam carry the stuff he'd brought in the plane.

Sam had brought Martha back from Fairbanks where she went to see the doctor, and he'd brought our mail in a big green sack.

Sam hollered at me when he came in the door. "Fred!" Sam White was big as Old Man Andreson and he always talked real loud. He put his hand on my head.

"Let me look at you! You grew some, didn't you?" I didn't know that I'd grown so I was happy to hear that.

They dumped everything from the mail bags on the floor so Old Man Andreson could sort it out. He was kind of stiff, Old Man Andreson, hard to bend over, so I helped him put everything in piles. I could read really good now, so I could be a lot of help to him he said.

Before he went back to his plane Sam put some money on the counter and took a candy bar out of the box behind the counter. A Baby Ruth. He gave it to me and said."Help you grow some more."

That Sam always does that. I'd take it home to share with Bokko.

There were two big boxes for the school from the library in Fairbanks. I could hardly wait to see what was in those. When Little Pete came in Old Man Andreson asked him to take the boxes to Miss Agnes in the wheel barrow.

Lots of people were coming to the store to see if they had any mail and to hear Old Man Andreson read the newspapers. So I went to Grandpa's to help him with the whitefish he caught in his net. Lots of whitefish in the fall, hardly anything else. I don't like cutting up whitefish because they have so many little bones that cut your hands. But they taste good.

When the whitefish first started running Grandpa gave a bunch to Miss Agnes to put it in jars so our cat could eat it all winter. He really, really liked whitefish. He purred the whole time he was eating it. I didn't see how he could purr and eat at the same time. And Jimmy wanted to know about how cats make that noise anyway, so Miss Agnes said she'd write to the library for a book about it for us.

Simon Luke was there helping Grandpa cut up the fish. He was even older than Grandpa and he used to tell us about when he was a reindeer herder. They're just like caribou, reindeer, just with a different name. A long time ago they gave a bunch of reindeers from somewhere far away to the people because they thought it would be better to raise them instead of going out to hunt caribou. It didn't work out very well, because the reindeer kept running away with the wild caribou herds and stuff.

Simon Luke had some good stories about how they used to stay out in reindeer camp and take care of them. I thought that would be a good thing to make a story about, so I asked him a lot of questions.

He liked it when us kids asked him stuff. Miss Agnes says we should always ask the old people questions because when they're gone their stories will be gone if we don't find out now.

That's bad to think about, stories gone forever.

I liked to make up stories, but I liked to write about the old days too. Like what Grandpa did when he was little, and about Old Man Andreson's life. Boy, he had some things happen to him. So when I went home that night I found a pencil and started writing about Simon Luke.

And when I read it out loud in school next day everyone liked it.

Chapter 7

Miss Agnes put up our old time line, the one we made last year. It stretched all along the wall under the blackboard and every time we learned something she'd make a picture about it at the right place. It started way back when people were just starting, like when they first got fire. And the last place was now, 1949. It was really good, seeing the story of the world stretched out like that.

10,000 was when people first started farming. Farming is not something the Eskimos and Indians in Alaska ever did. But I don't know why.

And then 8,000 is when people came to Alaska and then went all the way down to the end of South America. They came across where there was land and it's covered with water now but then it was land. And they kept coming and coming for thousands of years until there were people all the way down at the end of the tip of South America. And that's how people got all the way from Africa to here.

It was a good thing that people started in Africa because they didn't know how to make clothes. But that was okay because in Africa you don't need clothes. By the time they got to where it was cold they knew how to make clothes and that was good or else they would have frozen.

And then 4000 is when they invented the wheel. I always think about that guy who first made the wheel. Or the first guy who found out how to make a fire. You'd think everyone would think making fire instead of waiting for lightening or something was wonderful. Or that everyone would be just excited about wheels. But Miss Agnes said that there were probably a lot who thought the new things were stupid. Or like Grandma says, *hutlaanee*. Bad luck.

If I had a time machine that's what I'd really like to go back to see.

Miss Agnes said we'd have to write the books we read on the time line in red ink and the history dates in black so we wouldn't get get mixed up with what was real and what was made up in stories. Like last year we put *King Arthur* and *Robin Hood* on the time-line and those weren't really true. Just a little bit true.

When it was time for our first history lesson she said we were going to learn about Egypt on the top of Africa. Which happened way, way back on the time line. 6000. That's way before Rome that we learned about last year.

Six thousand years is hard to imagine. I can't even really imagine back before I was born, or when Grandpa was little.

She had those two boxes from the library little Pete brought her from the store and they were full of books about Egypt. She said the library in Fairbanks would send us boxes of books we needed, but we had to take good care of them because Sam had to take them back.

She said the Egypt people really liked cats. She showed us a picture in one of the books of a cat statue and the cat had a little earring in his ear, and a fancy collar. And he looked just proud of his jewelry.

While all us big kids were looking at those books Miss Agnes had the little ones start to make an Egyptian town with stiff white paper.

Those houses were made with mud. Just think. You could go to the river and get some mud and mix it up with chopped straw and put the mud in square boxes and the sun would dry the mud into bricks. And they'd build a house that way. Lots easier than cutting down logs like we do. And we have to go a long way away to get the right kind of logs, and in Egypt there was always mud right there.

I usually went to Grandpa's after school to tell him what we learned that day. Grandpa was always interested and so were his friends, the old men who drank tea with him. They never got to go to school much and Grandpa was the only one of them could read a little.

First I went in the dresser drawer and got out Grandpa's time line I made him last year out of some of Old Man Andreson's skinny paper he uses for his adding machine. I had to unroll it and put it flat on the table because Grandma doesn't like it pinned on the wall. I wrote down Egypt way down at the left side and made a pyramid too.

Then I told Grandpa and them about that mud the Egyptians had. Then Grandpa said some of the old people way down the Yukon used to mix mud with ptarmigan feathers and other stuff and bake it in the fire to make pots. I never heard about that before.

Mud is a lot more useful than I knew.

It looked like so much fun to make those Egyptian paper houses that all us older kids started doing it, too. The big boys were all teasing Marie about her house which was kind of wobbly. They all like to tease Marie because she never gets mad. She just laughs at them.

Pretty soon we had enough houses for a good village and we set it up on the table in the back. Those people got so hot that they slept on their roofs, and had little shade things to keep the sun off them while they slept.

We never get that hot here.

But our cat would jump on the table and bat at the houses with his paw so they'd all fall over, and the little people we made would fall off their roofs and we'd have to set it up again.

"He's just nuisance," said Selena.

Chapter 8

Every day I would take home a new book from the gas boxes to read.

I couldn't read until I was in bed because Mamma didn't think reading was really work, even when I told her what Miss Agnes said. That it was the most important thing.

Mamma works all the time. Cooking and sewing and working for Old Man Andreson and washing clothes and scrubbing the floors. And when we're home we work, too. Grandpa and Grandma say we're good workers, me and Bokko.

But still I wished I could read all day, sometimes. I really felt sorry for Jimmy, all those new books of ours, eight boxes, and he liked to read more than me, even, and he didn't have time. He was always studying for his test, and he couldn't take them home to read because it made his dad mad. Kind of like Mamma.

The first day the books were on the shelves I took *Boxcar Children* and that was the best book that ever was.

I always think the book I just read was the best book that ever was. And I make Bertha read the book next, because it's good when you share books like that. And can talk about the people in them like they were real.

But *Boxcar Children* was so good I read it over again before I gave it to Bertha. But I couldn't just keep reading the same book over and over because I had to read the rest of them in the shelves. So the next time I took *The Bobbsey Twins* and that was good, too, Freddie and Flossie and them. And Bert and Nan. They were all twins.

Roger's older brothers were twins, too. The kind that look just alike. Ivan and Arvin. But Ivan, he died in the river one year. I think it would be sad to be a twin and have your other part missing. And then Roger's mom had some more twins, but these ones didn't look alike.

Miss Agnes read to us every day when we ate our lunch.

We all usually had fish for lunch, salmon strips or half-dried fish. Miss Agnes didn't like fish so she always brought a peanut butter sandwich, but she ate it really fast and then she'd read while we ate. Walking back and forth in front of the window.

I was in charge of making the tea and Marie was in charge of getting the cups and pouring out our tea while Miss Agnes read.

Julia Pitka and Bertha's mom were at the school visiting our cat when she started our new book. It was *Black Beauty* and they stopped playing with our cat to listen. They got so interested that they came every day at lunch time to hear the story, to see how it came out. It was really sad, that book, because people were so mean to the horses.

People around here really like stories. Everyone listens to the radio stories at home at night, *The Lone Ranger and the Shadow*, and them. That's because before there was radio people used to tell stories every night. And Miss Toby says the storyteller always said at the end of the story, 'now we've chewed off part of the winter.' I like that. It's kind of like how the fairy tales say at the end 'happily every after.'

So when Julia and Amy found out about Miss Agnes' stories they couldn't stay away. They'd bring their knitting and watch Miss Agnes' face, like we did, their fingers just flying. When we finished that book, Julia took it home to read herself, even though she said she couldn't read very good. But Miss Agnes said the more she read the better she'd get at it, so Julia was glad to hear that.

In the morning us big kids worked at our desks while Miss Agnes worked with the little ones. But even when she was helping them we could bring her our work to correct. Like if I did an arithmetic problem I would bring it to her and she'd correct it while she was still reading with Charlie-Boy or something. She said you had to know if you had the right answer right away or else you wouldn't learn anything because you'd forget what you were thinking if you waited to find out. If it was wrong we'd go back and fix it and bring it to her again.

So while she was reading with Charlie Boy or Benny she'd also be correcting everyone's arithmetic problems. She could correct problems so fast you wouldn't believe it. And we could bring her our dictionaries so she could write a word in it to do our stories. Miss Agnes could do two or three things at once.

Jimmy Sam had a fat book for his arithmetic. Not just pieces of paper like us. He had the answers in back of his book so he'd look himself to see if he had the right answer. He was learning really hard arithmetic for his exam. With *letters* in it. Those problems looked so crazy it made me feel kind of sick to look at them. But Jimmy said that kind of arithmetic was fun.

All of us helped the little kids. Toby Joe and them had already taught Benny the alphabet, but he didn't know the little letters, so Miss Agnes made a game for him to match the little ones with the big ones, and we all played that with him when we had time. And we heard Selina and Charlie-Boy read, and helped them with their words if they needed something for their dictionaries.

Even Jimmy helped the little kids. And Bokko, too. He helped her a lot. He was just patient and always made them laugh when he helped them, even when they were feeling crabby about something being hard. I think he helped them so much, even he was so busy, because he liked explaining stuff. I told Miss Agnes that, and she said people who love to learn usually like to teach. She said there was a famous poem about a man that said, "gladly would he learn and gladly teach." I think Grandpa is like that too. Gladly would he learn and gladly teach.

And us big kids helped each other, too. Miss Agnes said the best way to really learn something was to teach it, and that was true because I helped Plasker with his hard multiplications, the kind that have those dots in it. Those dots make you crazy because they keep moving around. But after I explained it to Plasker I understood it a lot better.

In the mornings Miss Agnes would work with Bokko, too, on her writing. It was the little words that were hard for Bokko. When you're talking in signs you say, horse pretty. But when you write it you have to put in little words, like that horse is pretty. It was hard for Bokko to figure out those little words. Miss Agnes said it was hard for her to *explain* how come you needed them when you were writing.

She read the little kids stories, too, while we did our morning work. Like *Peter Rabbit*. Even if it was a baby story, us other kids liked it.

And she would teach them a lot of stuff like poems, *Hickory Dickory Dock* and all that. And we'd learn them right along with the little ones. We could hear everyone's lessons while we were doing ours and it didn't mix us up, so I guess we were like Miss Agnes and could do more than one thing at once.

Miss Agnes said that we had to know baby stories and rhymes because all the books we would read would talk about them and we wouldn't know what they were talking about if we didn't know the baby stuff. Like if a book said someone was like Humpty Dumpty that would mean that they'd gotten ruined some way and it couldn't be fixed. And if you never learned that rhyme about Humpty Dumpty you wouldn't know what that book meant, would you?

Last year Miss Agnes taught us little songs to help us memorize things. She said you could memorize anything fast if you sang it. Like the abc's, and the days, and the multiplication tables. We could all sing them. Even Selina and Charlie-Boy who just did adding and that could sing the multiplication tables last year.

This year she taught us a new song to remember the months by and another one about how many days they had. Because the months had different numbers of days.

But the only trouble with memorizing stuff that way is if you want to remember like when July comes you have to sing the whole song to yourself. Or with the abc's, if I want to remember if f is before g or after I have to sing the song from the very beginning. I sing it in my head, but still.

When she taught us the calendar songs Miss Agnes pinned up her Athabascan calendar next to our one Old Man Andreson gives us every year from the Pillsbury Flour. Miss Agnes made her calendar a long time ago when she was up at Allakaket.

There's no spelling for the Athabascan words, so Miss Agnes just wrote what they meant. Like, there was The Month Boats Are Put in the Water, and Month of the Hawk. The name I liked best was the one for January. Month of the Days Going from Short to Long. Because that's how it is in January. It's dark, dark winter, and then one day we notice there's sun on the tops of the trees, and then all of a sudden it isn't dark when we come to school. It always makes us feel crazy happy when that happens.

Then she showed us the calendar the Indians in Mexico made a long time ago. It's a circle.

Sometimes you think the way we do things is the only way, but that's not true. Everybody in the world has their own ways. And nobody's way is the right way.

But Miss Agnes says people sure get in lots of fights because they want their way to be the right way.

Miss Agnes had made beautiful pictures with water colors for her Athabascan calendar. When it was time for art we asked her to show us how to make pictures like that. Water colors are almost like magic because they nearly paint themselves. When you put water on the paper the colors run together. And look like the sky or the snow. Or like when the sun is setting .

Bokko liked painting and drawing more than almost anybody, once she got used to it. I think the best thing about painting and that for Bokko is that you don't need words to do it.

Last year every bit of space on the walls was covered with our pictures because Miss Agnes really liked our pictures.

The first day after Miss Agnes was back Little Pete made this good picture of a raven, with a white space all around the edges like Miss Agnes taught us to do. He made how the ravens have these kind of fingers on the ends of their wings and the kind of bend in their beaks. It was just perfect. Little Pete knows more about birds than anyone, I think. And Roger did one of the Lockheed Constellation Miss Agnes flew to England on. From the picture she gave him of it.

We all had pictures we wanted to make stuffed up in us from the summer. Like we had stories we wanted to write. So when we were back in school with all the good things to draw and paint with we made a lot, lot of pictures.

While we made pictures she played records for us on her battery record player. She said sometimes music was drawing pictures too, trying to show with the music what something looked like.

She played a record about a swan, and it was a song on a cello. That's a funny word, because the c doesn't sound like a c in our alphabet. Like a ch.

It really did sound like a swan if you see them swimming on the creek, smooth, like they didn't have little paddles under the water.

And then she played a record that was about a river. She said the man who wrote it lived far away in the country of Czechoslovakia. We learned that country last year. See, now it's cz that makes the ch sound.

The alphabet is not the same everywhere.

The river was the Moldau, and it was like the Yukon. The music started when the river was just a little creek like and got bigger on its way to the ocean, just like the Yukon. And louder.

We were so surprised that music could make pictures of something.

But Miss Agnes will never run out of things to surprise us with, I think.

Chapter 9

Miss Agnes was reading the little kids a book about an elephant called Babar. He lived in Africa. We all liked that story. And we liked it when Miss Agnes told us about the clothes Babar wore, like these white covers for the tops of your shoes. Miss Agnes said people wore stuff like that even when she was a little girl.

She drew us pictures of things like corsets that women wore to make their middle just tiny. And the corsets pushed their stomach and lungs and things all any which way. And then there were these big puffy things that women wore to make their butts look big. People sure can think up crazy stuff to wear.

One day Miss Agnes got a big book in the mail bag Sam brought. We all crowded around the long table to look at it. It was an animal book. Brand new. We never knew about hardly any of those animals.

That book was just fat and we thought it had all the animals in the world in it.

But Miss Agnes said that there were lots of animals in the world that weren't in the book, because there were too many animals for just one book. The kind that you couldn't see without a microscope. And the ones in the ocean that were like plants. Jimmy Sam was studying those for his test.

First she showed us the pages with all the cats. Like all the cats were in one family. There were a lot, lot of cats.

Jimmy was learning to put all the animals in this certain order Miss Agnes taught him that he'd need for his test. All the animals had a family, with a special name he had to learn. Jimmy liked our new animal book a lot because the books he was studying now didn't have many pictures. Just a lot of words.

Bokko wanted to know the signs for the animals she really liked, but most of the animals weren't in her sign book because they were not really popular animals. Like the okapi she liked because of the design on his legs, and this really fat thing called a manatee she liked. "Nice face," she signed, and it did have a sweet face. Miss Agnes said she'd write to Bokko's school and see if they didn't have a sign dictionary just for animals or something.

Miss Agnes said if you draw something you will never forget it. So she said when we were finished with our morning work we could go to the book and draw one of the animals that we liked and then Miss Agnes would put the picture on the big map to show where the animal lived. Some animals lived in just one place, like kangaroos, and some lived everywhere, like bats. Even we have bats here. Just little ones, but still.

We all hurried to finish our work fast because we wanted to draw all the animals we liked the best.

But Charlie-Boy just drew elephants every day. He said it was the best animal, because he liked that Babar book Miss Agnes had read them.

"Did you know there used to be elephants in Alaska, Charlie?" she asked him. Charlie frowned to show he didn't believe her. "Nah," he said.

"It's true," she said. "I'll get you a book from the library about them."

I could hardly wait to tell Grandpa about the elephants who used to live here.

But was I surprised, because he already knew about them. He told me about the ones they used to dig up when they worked in the mines over by the Hog River.

There are these big hoses that are supposed to thaw out the muck so they can get the gold out of it, and sometimes they would find something that had been frozen in there. Big old trees made of rock, and different skulls and once a whole beaver dam and some bones of a very, very big beaver.

And once the head of the old time elephants with big tusks lying broken next to it. Grandpa and them saw a lot of the tusks when they worked at the mines. And big teeth, like our teeth in the back of our mouths. But those teeth were really big, Grandpa said. Big as two fists.

And Grandpa said his mamma knew about those elephants too. She said they used to find those bones and the old people would tell them that those were the animals that lived underground. She said that was what people hunted in the world where the dead went, underground. Even when they were dead, those old time people had to hunt for food.

Miss Agnes started to teach us about orchestras. That's like the big band that played the music on the records she played us. She showed us a picture with all the people sitting in a sort of half circle, play-ing their music. We had to laugh, looking at all the people. When we have a dance or a potlatch or something we never have more than three people playing.

She told us the names of the instruments and how some were made of metal and some of wood.

Then she showed us a big picture of a clarinet, with all these curly parts and little caps for the holes. And then she played us a clarinet song. It's kind of whiney, the clarinet. But pretty.

She told us the story of the boy who wrote the song. He was Mozart and he wrote his first songs when he was the same age as Charlie-Boy. And he played them for kings on this instrument with a hard name that's got black and white keys on a shelf like. They were so excited that such a little boy could do that.

Miss Agnes drew a picture of him, Mozart, for the time line, fast like she always did, and there he was, a little boy playing his music in really tight clothes and with a wig. What if we had to dress like that? How could you even run or anything?

She put that picture at 1790 on the time line, and when Plasker's dad had a batch of new pups Plasker named the one with a white head Mozart. Because it looked like he had a wig, he said.

The sky got really gray and soft while we were in school. I think it looks like pussy willows then. So we all knew it was going to snow. I really like the first snow. It makes everything so cozy or something. When I went to the store after school it started to come down, little soft flakes.

Old Man Andreson had been baking in his little kitchen behind the store. He never made bread loaves the way our moms did. He just made pans of fat rolls. He said that way he didn't have to cut the bread to make sandwiches. He told me to sit down and have some so I had two with lots of butter melting off them they were so hot still. He's a good baker, old man Andreson.

He was listening to the radio and it was all about some war. Korea, he said. I couldn't exactly remember where it was on the map at school. Neither did old man Andreson.

"But it's in the north," he said. "It gets cold there. Hard to fight a war in the cold."

Then he said, "Well, what did you learn in school today, Fred?" He always asks me that. So I told him about the orchestra.

"I used to play the tuba," he said. I just stared at him. "You mean that big, big one?"

"Yeah. Not much to it. Few notes, that's all you play. We had a marching band when I was in school, before I run away to the gold rush. Had uniforms and everything. I played the tuba because I was the biggest and could carry it around easier than some of them skinny boys."

Next day in school I told everyone about Old Man Andreson and the tuba and we all laughed because it seemed like just the right thing for him to play.

I asked Miss Agnes about Korea and she told us there was a war there now. She put a pin on the map on Korea, and she wrote Korean War at the end of the time line.

"It seems like we just got finished with a war," Little Pete said.

"We will never be finished with war," said Miss Agnes.

Miss Agnes never gives us tests like our other teachers did. She just puts all the things we learn into the question box and then we have a quiz show every so often. Like she put the names of the Egypt cities and the river and all that on cards for our quiz show. There are a million cards in our quiz box now.

It's good because you never forget stuff. She had all the questions in there from what we learned last year, too, and she asked those to see if we'd forgotten anything, and we hardly ever did.

Sam listened to us once when we had a quiz show. He said we knew a lot more than him.

But I didn't really believe him.

Miss Agnes says you must keep learning all your life, and that's why we should read a lot. She doesn't think anyone is too old to learn anything.

At night sometimes Plasker's dad comes to Miss Agnes' house because Miss Agnes started teaching him to read and write last year. And Bobby Kennedy started to come this year, too, but he could read some so he didn't need to start with the alphabet and all.

Sometimes Bobby brought his mandolin and he and Miss Agnes would play together. Miss Agnes said the mandolin and the concertina don't really sound very good together because the concertina keeps drowning out the mandolin. But it was fun anyway.

Bobby is this crazy old guy who is just nuisance like Roger or one of the boys. Just full of the devil, Grandpa says. Once when Miss Agnes left the store Bobby told all the other people in there, "That's my girl friend."

He wouldn't have dared to say that while Miss Agnes was still there.

Chapter 10

The weekend after it snowed Mamma started her sewing.

Grandpa runs a little trapline out of the village and he brings her rabbit skins and marten skins to sew.

But he doesn't go out for beaver anymore. That's too much work because you got to chop holes in the ice when you set the traps and when you check them because the holes freeze over again. So Mamma got her beaver skins from other people.

But she was mad because she got two beaver skins from Amy Barrington and Amy had left fat on the biggest one when she skinned it. So it was really going to be hard to tan. Hard to scrape that dried-on fat off.

"That's lazy work. You girls remember what I tell you. Has to be just like a baby skin when you finish skinning. She don't know nothing, Amy."

Bokko and me were sewing *tilth*. That's rabbit socks for inside your boots. You put the fur inside next to your feet and it's really warm. But you have to make new ones every year because the fur would wear off. *Tilth* are easy to make because you don't have to be too careful. Not like boots and mitts which have to be perfect. I'm not good at that kind of perfect sewing, but Bokko is. She hardly gets her sewing sent back to her to do over, like I do all the time.

We were listening to the radio like we always do when we're home. It comes from Fairbanks, our radio, and that's where we learn our new songs. There's this one show for kids on Saturday that we like, too, and at night lots of stories about the Lone Ranger and them. And there are messages on the radio every night at nine, like when Martha went to town to see the doctor she sent a message back to her husband that she had to stay an extra day.

I wonder what it was like without radio in the old days.

Mamma was making a beaver hat for Jimmy's dad, Henry, because Henry didn't have a wife to sew for him. So Henry had to get Mamma and some other women to sew for him and his boys. But Mamma was the best sewer.

Grandpa told us our dad was just proud of Mamma's sewing. When he died of t.b. way down in Juneau they buried him down there. So Mamma couldn't dress him like they do when someone dies here, with all new clothes.

But Mamma made our daddy new boots and a marten hat and big moosehide mitts all covered with beads anyway.

They're in a box on our shelf.

Mamma told us Jimmy Sam's father was still crabby about how Jimmy wanted to go away to school. "Because your sons are supposed to help you when you're old," Mamma said. Mamma didn't think Jimmy should go away either. Or Bokko, really.

But Jimmy's father wasn't old even. And he had Paddy to help him. So I thought it wasn't fair to make Jimmy feel bad about wanting to be something different than a regular person.

Us kids were all excited about Jimmy's school and his test. We were just proud of him. And he never acted like he thought he was smart or anything. Lots of times he was quiet, like he was somewhere else in his head, thinking. But he didn't brag or anything.

Grandma got mad at us when we talked about Jimmy's test. That's *hutlaanee*, you make a bad thing happen by talking about it. Like if you're going hunting you never talk about it. Maybe you just say you're looking for a big thing. And that would mean a moose or bear. But it would be *hutlaanee* to say you're going to hunt a moose. Like bragging to the world. Or if you're going to have a baby you don't make clothes for it before its born. That's *hutlaa-nee*, too. Asking for bad luck. So Grandma said we shouldn't even talk about Jimmy's test.

We liked to watch what Jimmy was doing that was different from us, like that arithmetic in the fat book. Jimmy told us lots about stuff he was studying, too. When he learned something new he wanted to tell us about it.

Like he made a really nice time line for us about the animals he was studying. Jimmy's time line went up to the ceiling and down to the floor instead of across like our time line. There was a big space when there weren't any animals on the earth at all. And then a bigger space when there were just little animals you see in the microscope. And then right at the end a whole lot of animals were crowded together, like once they got started it got easier to make animals.

After animals got backbones it was fish first and then amphibians and reptiles and birds and mammals. We learned all those last year. It's the ones without backbones we didn't know about.

But Jimmy had all of them in his book and he learned the order they came in. He said them for us. That Jimmy could learn anything. He said there was a line like that for plants, from the beginning ones to the ones now, but he hadn't studied it yet.

By the time the second snow came our room looked really wonderful. It was bright because of the snow outside, and everywhere you looked there was something good, like our time-line and all the pictures pinned on the map, and the Egypt village, and Plasksar's Egypt gods.

Plaskar took one of the long pieces of paper Miss Agnes uses for the time line and made a whole row of all the different kinds of gods the Egyptians had. He thought they were the best thing about Egypt.

There was a cat god, even. His name was Bast. And one with a bird's head and a dog's head and lots of others.

The Egypt artists made all their people with sideways heads and frontways bodies. Miss Agnes said they didn't make the body sideways for three thousand years.

That's because artists had to copy each other. They couldn't try anything their own way. That's really crazy.

That was the worst thing about Egypt, I thought.

Little Pete looked for a long time at Plaskar's gods.

"There's just one now right?" he said finally. Miss Agnes looked a question at him, and he said, "Gods. There's just one now, isn't there?"

"Oh my no," she said. "There are still lots and lots. More than you can count. People all over the world have different gods."

"I didn't know there were different gods," Kenny said.

"One of the reasons people need an education is to learn that there are many, many ways of doing things and making things and thinking," Miss Agnes said. "People without an education think that their way is the only way and so they're upset when they come up against something different. For instance, in some countries people eat insects."

We all said oooh and ick when she told us this and Bokko looked at Charlie-Boy to tell her what we were all acting crazy about. When he signed it to her she made a face too. Miss Agnes laughed.

"And why not?" she said. "Just because it doesn't sound like good food to you doesn't mean it isn't."

I couldn't wait to tell that to Grandpa.

One day after Sam White had brought the mail old Man Andreson brought Miss Agnes a big square flat box. He was very excited and winked at us. "Now you'll see something," he said. Miss Agnes unwrapped the box and took out two big wheel things.

"These go with that big box in the closet that I told you was a secret," Miss Agnes said. " That's the projector, and these are the movie reels and Jack's going to set the projector up at the store so now we can all see this movie."

Marie nearly fell out of her chair and she just squealed. We could hardly believe it. Lots of people in our village had seen a movie when they went to Fairbanks. But none of us kids in school had ever seen one. Except Kenny went once when he had to go to the hospital but he was too little to remember it.

But we knew all about movies anyway because of the people who'd seen them in Fairbanks and because of Marie. The traveling nurse had given Marie some movie magazines about the stars and people who were in the movies and Marie used to look at those all the time. And tried to make her hair look like this one star.

"We'll show this one Friday night," said Old Man Andreson. "This here is a cowboy movie. Roy Rogers," he said.

Bertha and I were so excited we hugged each other. It was only Wednesday, and we didn't know how we could wait.

Chapter 11

The store was the only place to show movies because it was the only place that had electricity. Old Man Andreson had a little gas generator behind the store to run the lightbulbs in the store. That was the only thing he used electricity for.

I helped Old Man Andreson put a big sheet high up on the log wall behind the stove. It was supposed to be a white sheet, but the only one he had was kind of yellow. He stood on a chair and hammered some tacks into the sheet up at the top, and then we stretched the sheet real tight on the bottom so there wouldn't be any wrinkles, and nailed that part into the logs too.

There still were wrinkles though, because the sheet had been a long time on Old Man Andreson's top shelf. "I don't use sheets. Just sleep in my sleeping bag," he said.

He put the projector on a bench but when we tried it it wasn't up high enough to shine on the sheet. So he got two cases of canned milk for the projector to sit on and that was just right.

"Where's everyone going to sit?" I asked.

" You kids have to sit on the floor. I've got these two benches over here, and see if your grandpa will loan us those ones he has outside his door. And we'll tell everyone to bring a gas box."

Miss Agnes came early to help us, but by the time she got there nearly all the people in town had come, they were so excited to see a movie.

Bertha had a little box and everyone gave her their money for watching the show. Mamma was crabby about that, paying money for nothing, she said, but still she didn't want to stay home. There was Barney Sam and George and them and Clayton Malamute and Bertha's folks, and Old Man Toby and Sally Oldman and Grandpa and Grandma and Miss Toby and Martha and Bobby Kennedy and Martin Olin, Big Pete, almost all Roger's brothers and all the kids from school. And all the little kids who weren't old enough for school came with their mammas and grandmas. And those little kids were just terrible, running around and that until Old Man Andreson told the people to make the kids sit down or they'd knock the projector over.

Oh, everyone was there. Except some of the men were up the North Fork hunting. They would be very disgusted when they heard what they had missed.

Old Man Andreson had trouble putting the wheel thing on the projector, so Jimmy did it. Jimmy always knew how to work anything like a machine. He had to put the tape through a lot of little parts. It looked very hard to me.

Some of the grown-ups were smoking and the smoke went up into the beam of light from the projector. It twirled and turned there like little dancers. When Julia opened the door to come in the smoke dancers shrunk up and ran away, like they were scared to death. And then the smoke came right back to play in the light again. I thought I would write a story about that.

Then Jimmy turned on the projector and the reel began to turn, tickty-tickety. Old Man Andreson pulled the chain on the light bulb over his head so it would be dark.

All of a sudden the picture showed on the sheet, and the music blared out at us. We all jumped and held our ears til Jimmy turned the sound down.

It was wonderful. Like you were in the picture.

The horses had sad eyes like a moose. I would be scared to get up on one. There's this old guy called Gabby Hayes who did everything wrong and then all the grown-ups watching the movie would wrap their arms around their middles as if they might fall apart laughing. And Dale Evans was Roy Roger's girlfriend and she was really pretty and had a white cowboy suit on. With *pants*.

And every single person in the movie had these boots on with pointy toes. Cowboy boots are very ugly.

When we were at a really exciting part all of a sudden the screen was full of black numbers and the projector was going clackety clack really loud and the end of the film was flying around loose. We all jumped as if the projector had exploded and Roger's littlest baby sister screamed and screamed. Old Man Andreson said it was just time to put on another reel.

But first you had to rewind the first one, so Old Man Andreson pulled the light on and everyone talked all excited about the movie while Jimmy did that. It was just like a Louis L'Amour book, with bad guys and cowboys with these big pistols, almost as long as a rifle. I signed to Bokko some parts of the movie to be sure she knew what they were doing but I think she understood most of it.

When it was over we went out into the northern lights and they were really fast and a beautiful light green, but we weren't even seeing them, really. It was like when Miss Agnes reads to us we just go into the story. It was hard to come out of the place we'd been in the movie.

I was thinking how we'd never been anywhere, me and Bokko, just our own village, and now we could go lots of places in the movies. Like the magic carpet in that story.

Old Man Andreson said the next movie would be a cowboy one too. The people in Anchorage who sent out the films sent Old Man Andreson a big picture of that movie. It was "Red River" with John Wayne and showed pictures of those wagons with canvas on top and some painted Indians. Marie said John Wayne was really a famous movie person. Marie liked movie stars so much that old man Andreson gave her the picture of the John Wayne movie for herself.

As soon as we got to school on Monday we wanted to talk about that movie and we were full of a lot of questions for Miss Agnes. Seems like we all paid attention to the horses mostly because of that book, *Black Beauty*. We'd never seen a horse, just in pictures that don't move. Grandpa and them, they had lots of horses here in the old days at the mining camps but mostly they died of the cold, he said. He said the miners used them to pull their boats upriver, before they had kickers and that.

Roy Rogers had this horse called Trigger. I made a picture of Trigger but I couldn't get the color right. In the movie everything was black and white but Old

Man Andreson had a poster for that movie and Trigger was sort of yellow in that picture. But not really yellow. He was this color that wasn't even in our big crayon box. The one with forty-eight colors. I used the peach crayon, but I wasn't happy with it. Benny made a picture of Trigger too. But he colored his Trigger green.

Kenny drew the saddle that went on the horses. A saddle has lots of parts, and he did it good. He asked Miss Agnes why they had to put a blanket under it, and I knew the answer to that because of those Louis L'Amour books. She drew another saddle on the board and it was an English saddle she said. It was really small and thin-looking, that kind of saddle. I like the American one best because I would want to have that big horn to hold onto.

She drew another picture to show how women used to ride with both legs on one side because they had all those long skirts. That was really silly because you could fall off easy.

And she drew the harness thing that goes around the horse's head and a thing that goes into the horse's mouth. The bit. And you pull on the leather cord things on the bit to tell the horse which way to go.

Funny you don't put a bit in a dog's mouth. We wondered why they couldn't just put the cords on the side of the horse's head harness and just tug on the left one or the right one instead of putting in the bit. Or why you couldn't just tell the horse which way to go, the way we do dogs to make them go a certain way. Gee! Haw!

And Miss Agnes said she didn't know a single thing about horses because she was not raised in the country but when we found someone who knew about horses we'd ask them all those questions. And we'd see if the library could send us some books about horses. Miss Agnes had a long list of books she had to ask the library for because we asked so many questions. Miss Agnes loved our questions.

She said that meant we were thinking.

She said the questions she liked best were the ones she didn't know the answer to. Because when we found out the answer then she'd know something new too.

She said you didn't have to know everything, because no one could do that. You just had to know how to *find* the answers.

That was what school was for, she said, to teach you to ask questions. And then teach you how to find the answers. And when you knew how, you could teach yourself all your life.

Benny wanted to write a story under his picture of the green Trigger. He got me to print it on a piece of paper and then he copied it under his picture.

"Roy Roger's horse is Trigger. He has a long tail and hair on his neck only on one side." Benny looked up at me while I wrote that. "Why does it only grow on one side, Fred?" I just shook my head at him. I didn't know.

Benny didn't know yet that you had to put letters in a line so sometimes it was hard to read with letters all jumping around any which way. But he was proud of his story, and so was Toby Joe.

Every one of us wrote our story about the movie and Roy Rogers and Dale Evans, and after school all the kids were playing cowboys and me and Bertha got into a fight about who would get to be Dale Evans.

And I had to be Gabby Hayes.

Chapter 12

When I went to Grandpa's house after school he was starting to build a new dog sled, and Luke Simon was helping him.

Grandpa had cut the long pieces of birch for the runners and he was boiling those pieces to make them soft. He had a big oil drum in the yard to boil wood in. Like for the snowshoes he made. After the wood was soft he would put them on a bender thing he made a long time ago that would make the soft wood dry curved up at the ends. If you don't do it just right the bend will come out of the runners and they'll be just straight and dig into the snow.

"Who's it for?" I asked.

"For Clement Henry," he said. That's a guy in Huslia. Sometimes him and his family go to our fish camp with us.

"He wants to get in the race at Fairbanks. So I'm making a little light sled for him. A race sled."

I knew about that race. The men used to listen to it on the radio and be really happy when one of the guys from Huslia or somewhere on the Koyukuk would win. I didn't think it was very interesting.

The old men always talked about how small the dogs were now. When they were young they had big, big dogs. Just a few, not seven or eight like people now.

And those days people didn't ride on the sled. Sometimes they walked in front to break the trail. And sometimes they walked in front to steer the sled with a g-pole. But they almost never rode on the sled.

Grandma was tired of their talk. She said in the summer all the men ever talked about was fish, fish, fish, and in the winter all they ever talked about was trapping and driving dogs. And that was true, they did.

Lots of people came to school to get books now. Old Man Andreson got one that was about inventions and he was crazy about that book. It told how things were invented and when. Like zippers and safety pins and windows and can openers. He was always talking about that book. I bet everyone in town is going to read it after him.

Miss Agnes taught us a new song from Australia that we all liked to sing really loud. "Waltzing Matilda." It had a lot of different words that they use in Australia, like billy is what you cook coffee in. But Miss Agnes told us what they all mean, so we knew. That's just like us, the way we have different words for things, like kicker for the engines and chickens for spruce hens and mush for oatmeal.

It was kind of a sad song, too, because this old guy didn't want to get sent to jail because he was hunting at the wrong time. It's the same here. You got to only hunt when the game wardens say you can, and if you get caught with something you're not supposed to have you could go to jail.

Like one Spring Clayton Malemute got a moose that he wasn't supposed to get, but moose hardly every come down this way so he just shot it anyway. And when the game warden flew in to tag beaver that day Clayton's mom Angela threw a whole big pot of moose head soup in the snow behind the house so the game warden guy wouldn't know about the moose. Boy, she was mad to throw away all that good soup.

Our ginger tom was really crazy sometimes. He'd jump up by the wash basin and dip his paw in the water like he was looking for a fish. And sometimes he'd knock things off the table just so he could look down to see them fall. Marie said that was just like what babies do, drop things on the floor for fun and wait for you to pick them up.

Only he didn't want you to pick them up, he wanted to jump down on the floor and skitter them around and chase them.

One day Kenny's beaver hat fell off the hook onto the floor, and our cat curled right up in that hat with his paws over his nose. He just loved it. So every day Kenny would put the hat on the windowsill for him to sleep in.

And Kenny said it was nice to have a warm hat to put on when it was time to go home.

Chapter 13

When it started to get dark out early Miss Agnes put some star charts up on the wall and showed us how the old people a long time ago used to think the stars made pictures. That's how they did around here, too, because Old Miss Toby and them told us some of the stories about stars. The Indian stories weren't anything like the ones Miss Agnes told us, because they were about hunting and that.

Miss Agnes said that every different kind of people all around the world had their own stories for the stars. We had to learn these stories that the Romans made up because when we read books they would talk about them and we'd have to know their names. Because no one else but us knew about the Athabascan stories.

We put all the star pictures in a little book we made and we were supposed to go out at night and see if we could find them. There was one that looked like a W. And there was the Big Dipper that kind of pointed at the North Star. We all liked that one because it was just like the dipper we all used at home to get water out of the water barrel. And there was a little dipper. Miss Agnes said some places they called those the little bear and the big bear.

My best was the Seven Sisters, a little bunch of stars together. I wrote a story about them, and what their names were and if they ever fought like me and Bokko do sometimes. But not very much.

The boys liked the one about the hunter, of course, and he had three stars in his belt. And the thing that held up his shirt thing was almost the biggest star in the world. In the universe, I mean. It was way, way bigger than the sun, which is really a star too. It was called a French name that sounds like beetle juice, which is a very funny name for a star.

When I told Grandma and Grandpa about those star stories Grandma looked cross. " Those aren't the right ones she's teaching you," she said. So she drew some different ones and told me the story. Miss Agnes asked Grandma to come to class to tell us all the old Athabascan star stories, but Grandma wouldn't. So Miss Agnes asked old Miss Toby to come and tell us, and Marie told us what she said.

Jimmy said the Athabascan story for the big dip-per was better because they just called it The One

That Goes Around. Because the big dipper turns in a sort of circle all winter.

Jimmy was studying a book about stars and that stuff for his science test. About what they're made of and how they start and all.

When Miss Agnes told us all the stuff in Jimmy's book we were not even surprised at all the things there were to know about stars. With Miss Agnes this is how it is about anything. The things you think are just ordinary, like stars, turn out to be complicated.

Like the big map. First there's the big part, and then you go down smaller and look at every country. And then you go smaller and every country is cut into smaller parts and then even smaller parts, like cities and that. And then even smaller. The kind of dirt they have and the kind of trees and things. It just gets smaller and smaller. It makes you think that nothing is just what it is. Nothing is simple.

I told that to Miss Anges and she said when she was a little girl all the kids wrote their address in their books like this. On the board she wrote

Agnes Sutterfield
26 Brixton Lane
Cambridge
Cambridgeshire
England
Great Britain
Europe

Northern Hemisphere
The Earth
The Solar System
Milky Way Galaxy
The Universe

See, small first and then the biggest. Or you could do it the other way, biggest first and then smallest.

We all liked that so much we started to write our own. I wrote mine in the front of my new writing book. Only we put in North America for our continent, and the United States for our country.

We had the map stuffed full of animals we all drew when we had time.

I was thinking and thinking about all the different kinds of animals and it seems like some of them are kind of a mistake. There are some really ugly animals out there. Like the hippopotamus. And the rhinoceros. Miss Agnes says if I think they are ugly just wait til I see some of the animals that died out before there were any people. Some of them were really terrible looking. We'll be learning about them later, she said.

Another thing I don't think is pretty is horses. Even though they're always talking in books about how beautiful they are. They have this big bulge on their cheeks and their butts are really big. And I don't much like the way their teeth look either.

I told that to Miss Agnes and she said, "Beauty is in the eye of the beholder." She said that means that everyone thinks different things are pretty. That's how come people have different favorite colors and all.

Thinking about that makes me feel kind of lonesome, like I'm all alone in my head.

Some birds are really pretty, and some snakes and some fish, but there are some ugly ones, too. I think the only animal that's pretty all the way, all the cousins and everyone in the family is cats. All cats are pretty. Maybe that's why the Egyptians liked them so much.

Miss Agnes had lots of questions in the question box about the instruments. First she'd show us the card with a picture of the instrument and we'd try to remember the name. And then she'd play us a little bit of an instrument on a record and we had to tell her what instrument made that sound. Some of them were easy, like the piano. But some were hard to tell apart, like the oboe and clarinet. Mostly they were easy, though.

One thing about the music Miss Agnes teaches us. Most of the time I don't feel bad that Bokko is deaf. But I feel bad that she can't hear the music. I think I like music better than almost anything. And I want Bokko to hear it too.

Instruments come in three kinds. The kinds you hit, and the kinds you blow into and the kinds that have strings. One day she played us a record story about a boy who was magiced to Orchestraville and he could play any instrument he wanted to right away without practicing. We really, really liked that one and we got Miss Agnes to play it for us lots. We wrote a lot of stories about that record.

I would like to play the trumpet. It sounds so loud and happy. But Miss Agnes said that if we want to play something it's never going to be magic. It's going to be hard work.

A lot of people around here play things. When all the miners were here when Grandpa was young they learned to play from them. Guitars and fiddles and Bobby Kennedy has a mandolin. And Jake, Bertha's dad, has a banjo, but it doesn't have any strings and no one knows how to play it. Those all have strings. Just Miss Agnes plays a thing you hit. Not really hit but press.

Of course most of the boys liked the drums. I don't know why boys always like really noisy things.

The really big fat one in the orchestra is called the kettle drum. That would be fun to play, I think.

Then Miss Agnes said in some places people use gas drums for their drums and they can play anything on them. Tunes and everything. We were really interested in that.

So Miss Agnes said she'd get a gas drum record for us next summer when she went on her vacation.

To play for us next year.

When she said that we all looked at each other. Bokko looked around at all of us, wondering why we all looked so happy. I signed Miss Agnes to her, that's an a over the forehead, and then I signed coming back.

Bokko must not have believed me because she looked at Charlie-Boy, because he's the best signer. And he signed the same thing, so Bokko looked happy then, too.

Miss Agnes was going to come back.

All year we'd been afraid to ask her, and here she'd been meaning all the time to come back for another year.

We thought she came back just to get Bokko and Jimmy off to school but she came back for us too.

I felt so good I thought I was going to burst.

Chapter 14

When we were finished with Egypt Miss Agnes told us about the other places in Africa. It's just like how Alaska belongs to the United States. Most of the African countries belong to other countries. Not to themselves.

So there are a lot of languages there. In Africa. The Eskimos have two different languages. And in Alaska the Indians speak a lot of different languages. My grandma can't understand people from way down river. Or from Ft. Yukon way upriver. And they can't understand her. But mostly everyone speaks English too.

And in Africa, like if France owns a country, most of the people speak French. And their other languages, too. And when the Russians owned Alaska most people could speak some Russian. Grandpa says his father could speak Russian really good because all the white people were Russians when he was a little boy.

Miss Agnes says a lot of things are the same around the world.

She taught us a song in a Africa language. It was so fun to sing.

I was thinking that the best songs go up and down a lot and surprise you. Like this Africa song. And like "Little Liza Jane." That one jumps all over the place. Songs that stay in one little space aren't as much fun to sing.

We didn't know what the words meant in this song and neither did Miss Agnes, but she knew it was about a lion hunt. And at the end you're supposed to raise your spear and say hah, really loud, and that's when you kill the lion. Because lions are like bears to them and people try to keep them away from their cows. I wish they didn't have to kill them because I like all the cats.

In that Africa language they put a m and a b together like for one sound. And they have another sound that's like a click. I wish I could do it, just click in the middle of a word. But I can't.

Miss Agnes says there's a sound in Athabascan that she could never make because she wasn't raised with the language. It's like a l and a th together. We can all say it because we heard it from when we were babies. Like *tilth*.

Miss Agnes says every language has sounds like that that are hard for strangers to say. She says if we listen carefully we'll hear that all the people in our village who talked Athabascan when they were babies, they can't say the th in English. Like they say dat instead of that. She says th is one of the hardest sounds in English. Really even some of us in school, we say d for th too, sometimes.

When people have a sound they can't say good, that's what people call an accent. Like Dominic, downriver. He's from that boot place on the map. Italy. And so he says his English with a different sound. He has a Italy accent. And Miss Agnes has a English accent. She can't really say r very good.

I think languages are very interesting.

After we sent back the Egypt books we got a lot of books from the library about Africa. There were a lot of National Geographics about Africa too, and I took one to Grandpa nearly every day.

Grandma doesn't like them, though. "What kind of people!" she always says. She doesn't like the clothes that people wear in other places and she doesn't like it at all when they don't wear any. So she frowns at me when I bring one to Grandpa.

I told Miss Agnes about how Grandpa and his old men really like to look at those National Geographics and so she gave me a map for Grandpa's wall. So they could find the places the stories are about. It's just a little map, but it shows the whole world. And Grandpa and them were just happy to have it.

We had mostly cowboy movies the rest of the winter. Hopalong Cassidy was the best one. He has a black horse. Miss Agnes wondered why we were always on the cowboys' side and not the Indians, because after all we were Indians. We just stared at her. Finally Plasker said, "Those are *bad* Indians."

"Hmm," said Miss Agnes. She put her eyebrow up really high. "I think we'd better study some American history soon."

Indians were named Indians even they don't live in India because of Christopher Columbus. Miss Agnes told us about that last year. Because Christopher Columbus was trying to get to India and he thought he had so he named the people Indians. So we are called Indians.

Miss Agnes says in England they call the Indians in North America Red Indians to be different from those people in India. That's very silly because I don't know anyone who is red.

But now all the native people in Alaska are called either Indians or Eskimos. Which are not the names they choose for themselves. I will be glad to learn more about Indians and especially what the real names are supposed to be.

Lots of times we'd get so interested in stuff Jimmy was studying for his exam we'd ask Miss Agnes to teach us about it.

One week she read us Shakespeare stories from the book Jimmy was studying for his test. Anyway, they're really plays but they wrote them up in a book like stories because the words of the plays are too old-fashioned to read if you don't know how. The boys thought it was funny to name someone Shake Spear.

Miss Agnes said Shakespeare is the most famous writer in England and that lots of people know his plays by heart. Even with the old-fashioned words. She said some part of a play for us, and then she told us what it meant because we couldn't understand one thing she said.

She read us the one about Romeo andJuliet, and about the old man who had three daughters and he was mean to the best one. And about these people who were shipwrecked on a dessert island.

I don't see why he's so famous because I didn't like any of those stories, but Marie liked the one about Romeo and Juliet because she always likes love stories.

Chapter 15

When the weather got cold our clothes hooks were just full up of parkas and mitts and hats and stuff. Our ginger tom would scramble up all the clothes and sit on the top shelf over the hooks. You could tell he thought he was smart to get so high up.

But he hated it when the cold white air came boiling into the room when someone opened the door. He'd flatten himself against the floor with his ears back and run into the book room. We all laughed when he did that, he looked so funny.

After there was enough snow for the dog sleds everyone was getting ready to go out to the trapline for marten.

I could tell Miss Agnes was not happy having Jimmy miss school to go trapping. Usually she tells us that going to the trapline is just another kind of school.

But with Jimmy being so short of time to learn for his test it was not so good. But he had to go and Paddy too, because that's how they got money to buy gas and the stuff at the store.

Miss Agnes packed up a bunch of books for Jimmy to read out there. He looked pretty worried when he saw them. I bet because he knew there wasn't going to be much time for studying. And because his dad would be mad.

When Miss Agnes saw him look like that she said, "Never mind." And she took the books back.

"You could use a vacation," she said. "Just memorize that list of dates and work on your parts of speech."

Parts of speech are the names words have to tell their jobs. Like the adjectives' job is to tell what something's like. Miss Agnes said we don't have to know them, but Jimmy had to. Because they'd be on his test.

Jimmy just nodded, but I know he was worried about how he was going to learn all this stuff for his test when he wasn't even going to be here again until Christmas. Because that's what I was worried about.

Roger and Little Pete and Toby Joe's families were going to their traplines too. Me and Bokko never go, because we don't have a dad, and Grandpa is too old. Me and Bokko are usually the only ones who stay in school all year, really.

Kenny and Plasker's dads went to work at the canneries down by Anchorage when winter came, so Kenny and Plasker wouldn't have to leave school for marten trapping. Not until beaver trapping season when their dads came back.

And Bertha's dad wasn't going trapping this year because he had a broken leg and he still couldn't walk all that much. He was pretty worried about not making any money trapping, but Old Man Andreson told him to start making snowshoes like Grandpa did, and he could make some money that way. Because Sam would sell them in Fairbanks. Bertha's dad wasn't that good at making stuff like that so Grandpa was helping him learn.

Marie's family went to the trapline every year but they always left her home to take care of the little kids. There was a new baby, born last summer and two real little ones.

And she was taking care of Benny, too, because he didn't want to leave school. Toby Joe's mamma said Benny just cried and cried and begged to stay because he was just learning to read. And he was afraid if he went trapping he'd forget how. So Marie told Toby Joe's mom that she'd keep Benny.

Grandpa says Marie is very good-hearted.

Marie could do everything a grown woman could do even if she was only fifteen. But she never got much time in school. So she wasn't as good at reading and writing as me and Bertha and the younger ones because we all spent more of the year in school.

Miss Agnes told the boys to write in their notebooks every day to keep in practice and she gave them books to read, too. Because reading and writing were the most important things to be good at, and if you were good at those you could learn everything else when there was time.

So Roger and Little Pete and Jimmy were gone trapping, and Toby Joe, and there were just eight of us left in school. But they'd be back before Christmas.

Still, we missed them. The big boys are so funny.

And Marie could only come sometimes if Sally Oldman would watch the little kids for awhile.

But Miss Agnes told Marie she'd help her write letters to the movie stars and we never saw Marie so excited about anything. Every day she'd write a letter and bring it for Miss Agnes to correct even if she had the little kids with her, and then she'd write it again and Miss Agnes would mail it for her.

And Miss Agnes had Sam get Marie a whole bunch of those movie magazines in Fairbanks they sold at the drugstore.

So Marie was doing a lot of reading and writing, too, even she wasn't in school. Just like the boys.

Chapter 16

Before everyone left to go trapping Miss Agnes read us these old stories in a book called *Arabian Nights*. There was this really good story about a magic cave, and you said "Open Sesame!" to get the door to open up.

And the best one was Aladdin. Miss Agnes said we would do our Christmas play about Aladdin and his magic lamp when everyone came back for Christmas.

Last year we did *A Christmas Carol* for our school play. It's about this old man who is mean and who gets nicer when these ghosts come. That was a really good one.

But Aladdin would be really good, too, because it would be so much fun to wear those clothes from Arabia.

Miss Agnes brought us a whole lot of this really thin curtain stuff, almost like mosquito net, only white. Bertha's mom Annie sewed these really fat pants for costumes out of that mosquito net stuff. Annie had a sewing machine and she made all of them in one day, she's so fast. Miss Agnes gave her the picture.

And the girls had veils that covered some of their faces but you could see through them.

Marie was going to be the princess and she was just excited when she saw the costume she would wear. And everyone would get to paint these dark lines around their eyes and wear a lot of jewels and stuff.

After everyone left to the trapline us kids who were staying in school worked every afternoon for awhile on the Aladdin play.

Miss Agnes showed us how to make things with old newspapers she got from Old Man Andreson. We tore up all the newspapers into little strips and she mixed some flour and water together into paste.

Then she showed Selina how to make made beads with that paper and paste. And after Selina painted them she rolled the beads in this sparkly gold stuff Miss Agnes had. Our cat was full of that gold stuff, in his paws and all over. I think he rolled in it. And we all had some on us even after we washed our faces. Even Miss Agnes had some in her hair. She said every time she used that gold stuff for something she told herself she'd never use it again, it made such a mess. But she always did.

Selina made so many beads Miss Agnes told her to stop and make some big jewels instead to put on the turbans. And we'd save some of the beads for our Christmas tree.

Then me and Plasker and Kenny made these big jugs with those newspaper strips. That's what they used in those countries long ago. Like we use wooden barrels. They weren't the whole jug, just half of it. But it looked like the whole jug was there when you put them against the wall.

Miss Agnes says when you put on a play you just have to make an illusion. That means things don't have to be really real.

And Bokko made a magic lamp with a curvy handle out of that newspaper and paste, and she painted it with a little can of gold paint Miss Agnes had. It was really beautiful.

We got some big pieces of cardboard from Old Man Andreson's cache. Old Man Andreson never throws anything away. Those were to paint the scenes of the market and the cave and the palace. Kenny and Plaskser did those. And me and Bokko and Selina painted these big pieces of canvas Old Man Andreson had, to look like fancy rugs that hang in the market place. Because that was what those Arabs were famous for. Rugs.

And Miss Agnes cut a bunch of circles out of thick cardboard and she had little Benny and Charlie Boy paint them with what was left of that gold paint. Those were gold coins for the magician to give Aladdin. They were so proud of those gold coins Miss Agnes said they could keep them when the play was over.

I thought the market was going to be the best scene with the rugs and those big jugs because in the cave it was going to be dark and all.

But Bokko thought the cave would be best because there were so many jewels lying around.

All the boys were supposed to wear turbans. Those are long cloths wrapped up into a hat thing. Miss Agnes made them turbans out of some of the old curtains. But they kept getting unwrapped. After that happened about a hundred times Miss Agnes got this idea to make them stiff so they couldn't fall apart. She made a big washtub full of starch and we put those turbans in there really easy and took them out again and then they dried hard and stiff and didn't fall apart any more. There are a lot of problems you have to figure out when you put on a play.

When we were finished making all the stuff us girls went to Miss Agnes' cabin after school one day and we made a lot of cookies for the Christmas play. Those cookies were delicious. There were three different kinds and we all got to try one of each before we put the cookies outdoors to freeze. One year Miss Agnes said she made cookies up at Allakaket where she was and she put them outside in a cardboard box and the camp robbers tore that box apart and took every cookie. Those birds steal just everything.

So we put our cookies in a gas can because even camp robbers couldn't get into a gas can. And then we hung the gas can from a tree limb because shrews and them could get into the gas can if there was even one hole. That's how everyone around here keeps stuff away from animals and them. Hang it in a tree.

Of course most everyone has a cache in town. That's a little cabin on tall poles so the animals can't get your stuff and chew it up. You have to make tin cans flat and nail them all around the poles so nothing can shinny up the poles and get into the cache. But if you don't have a cache you can just hang stuff in a tree.

Everyone was late getting back from the trapline because the weather got so bad. When it's forty and fifty below no one likes to travel if they don't have to. It's bad for the dogs. They might get stove up.

So when everyone finally got back from the trapline we had just a few days for everyone to practice what they had to say for the play.

I was the narrator. And the curtain puller. I just stood by the side of the stage and told what was happening. I got to wear a costume and beads and even I had a veil. But it kept getting in my mouth when I talked so I had to take it off.

Miss Agnes said having a narrator is a good thing to have when everyone didn't have a lot of time to practice. That way if they forgot something I could whisper and remind them what to say.

Everyone came to our play just like they did for the movies. And they really liked it, too. They laughed so hard when they saw the boys in those puffy curtain pants that they were almost falling off the chairs.

Kenny was Aladdin and Plasker and Toby Joe were his friends in the market place and of course Little Pete was the genii to come out of the lamp because he was the tallest one. Like last year he had to be Bob Cratchitt because he was the tallest. And Little Pete had this flashlight under his chin so it made him look really scary when he stood up over the lamp. And Miss Agnes had some blue powder, if you got it wet it would make a blue smoke and that was for Little Pete, too. Roger made the powder smoke when Little Pete was supposed to come out of the lamp. Everyone watching our play just screamed the first time it happened.

Marie was the beautiful princess Aladdin wanted to marry and Jimmy was her father the emperor who didn't want Aladdin to marry the princess because he was poor. Jimmy was so good, talking in this deep voice and acting mean. And Bokko was the emperor's wife.

I think Bokko was the best because she always talks with her face anyway, and that's good in a play.

And afterwards we put our regular clothes on and sang our Christmas songs and we all had hot cider like we did last year and the cookies we baked.

When it was New Year's we had a dance, and Miss Agnes taught everyone to sing this one song they sing in England at New Year's. "Auld Lang Syne," it's called. It's really sad, because it's a song about all the people you love who are gone. And I knew Miss Agnes had a lot of people to miss and so did me and Bokko and so did everyone.

I told Grandpa about that song and he said it's not just people you miss, it's your old life and the things you used to do before things changed.

Sometimes I think it must be sad to be old.

Chapter 17

A little after Christmas was beaver trapping time. Some of the kids went out to the traplines with their families, but not all of them. Roger's dad and Plasker's trapped beaver close to the village and so Plaksker and Roger weren't gone from school. Just Little Pete and Jimmy and Kenny and Toby Joe were gone. And Jimmy only stayed out with his dad for a few weeks, so that was good.

Beaver skins are a lot of work. After you skin the beaver you have to stretch the skins perfectly round, and nail them on a big board with a lot of tiny little nails. When they dry out you can take the skins off the board and stack them in a corner, but until then you have this whole house full of beaver skins drying on their big boards. Which don't smell good. Then in April the game wardens come and tag all the beaver so people can sell them and then Old Man Andreson sends them off to the fur buyers and it's all over for another year.

One good thing about beaver season is that everyone has a lot of beaver to eat, and they are really, really good. I would never get tired of beaver like I do of rabbit.

One day in March when the cold, cold days were nearly over and everyone was back from beaver trapping Sam came to our school. With a letter for Miss Agnes. We knew the way he acted that the letter was important, and that's why he didn't leave it at the store for Miss Agnes to pick up after school.

She kind of stared at the envelope while she held out her hand for Roger's pocket knife. Which she borrowed about a hundred times a day.

"From Jimmy's school," she told us. We all watched her while she sliced open the envelope, really careful, and we watched her face while she read it. But we couldn't tell anything from her face.

Then she read it to us.

The letter said they had found someone to give the test to Jimmy. We knew the test person would be from somewhere else. Somebody strict. Because like if Miss Agnes or Old Man Andreson gave the test to Jimmy, they might cheat for him. But we didn't know before who it would be. The letter said the priest at Allakaket would give the test. His name was Father Kirby.

"Do you know him?" I asked Miss Agnes, because she used to teach there, at Allakaket.

"No," she said. "He's someone new, since I left."

Father Kirby would come to our village in April and give Jimmy the test.

Miss Agnes pushed her fingers through her hair when she read us that part. It was not a very long time to April.

"We'll have to work faster," she said to Jimmy. He didn't say anything, he just nodded. But I think he felt like us, like it got real when that letter came. It was really going to happen, that test.

I really worried about that test. One day when I was helping Miss Agnes after school I said, "What will happen if Jimmy doesn't pass the test?" Miss Agnes didn't look at me, she just kept wiping the blackboard. "Can he take it again next year?" I asked. Then I answered myself. "His dad won't let him stay in school another year, will he?"

Miss Agnes looked at me then and tucked her mouth in at the corners like she does when something is bad.

I thought she was as worried as I was. How could Jimmy just leave school and be a regular person, with all the things that were in his head. With all the things he wanted to know? Like what if that Michael Farraday had to quit working on electricity and go back to his dad's blacksmith shop? But I didn't want to ask her any more and make her sad.

But there wasn't even as much time to study for the test as we thought there was. Old Man Andreson came to school to tell Miss Agnes that the priest had called him on the radio. He had to come give the test before the last week in March because he had to leave Allakaket to go to a big church meeting. The priest said one of the men there would bring him with dogs because it wasn't too far and the trail was really good this time of year. And that he'd be there on the next Monday for sure.

Miss Agnes and Jimmy just looked at each other for a minute.

"Only one more week," she said. There were some things Jimmy hadn't studied yet, because of going trapping and all. But Miss Agnes said they weren't as important as the other things, like science and math, which he'd studied hard.

Like there were these little ladder things you had to build out of a sentence with the words in the sentence on the right place in the ladder. It was really crazy looking and I didn't know one thing about it. Miss Agnes said it was very silly, pulling sentences apart like that, and that's why she'd put it off to last. And now there wasn't any time.

And also he'd never learned all the stuff about plants.

But Miss Agnes said, "Don't worry. You don't have to know *all* the answers. Just enough." And Jimmy nodded.

ButI think Jimmy and Miss Agnes were worried anyway because they had that tight look on their faces a lot.

Monday afternoon we were all listening for the priest to come. You can hear really good when the snow gets hardcrust like that. And the snow is off the trees. But I don't know why we were listening because we knew all the dogs in town would know they were coming a long time before we did. Dogs can hear anything from a long, long way off.

So we all jumped up to look every time a dog barked. We were just about wore out waiting. But finally it wasn't just a few dogs talking to each other, it was all the dogs, barking and looking upriver. Pretty soon we could hear the driver yelling to his dogs. And then we could see the team, a little line far down the river closer and closer, louder and louder.

Jimmy put on his parka and stuff to be ready to meet them. And Little Pete and Roger got dressed, too, to go help with the dogs.

The team pulled up the bank and stopped right next to the school. So much noise from our town dogs and the team dogs you could hardly think. Our ginger tom was sitting on the window sill but when he saw that dog team he jumped off and ran to the book room, faster than we ever saw him run, his tail just fat. He never came out of there the rest of the day, either.

All of us just crowded into the windows to look at this priest. He was all covered with frost, and so was Caleb John, who brought him from Allakaket. Caleb John was Little Pete's Uncle, his mamma's brother.

Caleb and the priest came into the school to warm up. Caleb John was almost as tall as Little Pete we saw.

When the priest pulled his parka hood down to thaw the ice on his eyebrows and eyelashes we all looked hard at him to see if he was nice. But we couldn't tell.

Miss Agnes took away the books that were piled up on the extra chairs so Caleb and Father Kirby could sit next to the fire and get warm. Then she nodded to Marie to pour tea for them.

Caleb was telling us what a hard time they had. They left early when the crust was hard and the trail was perfect. And then they came to a place where a moose walked in the trail and punched big holes in it and the dogs had a hard time with that ruined trail. So it took a lot longer to get to us than they thought.

"Lots of overflow, too," said Caleb.

Caleb told Little Pete about all the people in Allakaket that were related to Little Pete, and told

Miss Agnes about all the people in Allakaket that Miss Agnes knew from teaching there. Caleb had brought a bunch of letters to Miss Agnes that people in Allakaket had written to Miss Agnes. All the people she'd taught in school and them. They must miss her.

And the priest was looking around, at our pictures on the wall and trying to talk to us kids. But we were shy with him.

I think he liked our pictures.

They would have the test the next day. So Little Pete took his Uncle Caleb to his house to eat and all, and feed the dogs. And Jimmy took Father Kirby off to Annie and Jake's to spend the night. Because they were the only ones had an extra bed.

The next day the priest and Jimmy got ready to go to Miss Agnes' cabin to start the tests. Miss Agnes told them to hang a towel on a nail by the porch door and then she'd know they needed tea or something to eat. Otherwise no one was supposed to bother them.

Before he went out Jimmy picked up our cat. "Give me luck, you ginger tom," he said.

We all watched for that towel. Every time they put it out Miss Agnes would send some of us over with tea, or sandwiches when it was lunchtime. And she had a big pot of caribou stew she'd made for them on the back of our school stove. "You can't think when you're hungry," Miss Agnes said.

All of us who brought tea or sandwiches over there would come back and tell Miss Agnes how Jimmy looked. I thought he looked fine when it was my turn. Just smiled at me like he always does. And shook his hair out of his eyes, like he always does.

But when we went there we couldn't talk to Jimmy and he couldn't talk to us. Which was silly because even if he asked me the answer to a question on the test I wouldn't know it anyway, would I?

And then when they were finished eating and stuff they'd go to the next test. There were six of them, and he had an hour to do each one. The last one was the writing test. When that one was finished Jimmy would come to school to tell us about the test.

We all stayed late at school, waiting for him. We were so jumpy that Miss Agnes took out the book she was reading out loud at lunch time and read us two chapters. *Peter Pan*. And that is one of the best books because those kids could fly. But we still felt jumpy.

When he came in we looked all worried at Jimmy, but he just smiled at us. He fell into his desk and pretended he was all winded. To make us laugh. But he looked really funny in his face and I knew he was not really feeling like laughing himself.

We all had some tea and then he told us about the test.

"It was hard all right," he said. "The thing is, they give you choices. A,b,c,d. That's hard because first it looks really easy. But then you think it's sort of like a trick and maybe you're wrong. And then you feel all confused. It would be easier if you just wrote down the answer out of your head and didn't have any choices. So I kept going back and erasing. And then I'd run out of time."

"What about the things you didn't have time to study?" Little Pete asked.

"There wasn't any thing about plants in the science test. But there was some of that geometry we didn't study yet. I just guessed. And there was some of that diagramming. I just guessed on that, too."

Miss Agnes nodded as if it was just what she thought would happen.

"What about your essay?" she asked.

"I *think* I did it in good English." Jimmy looked worried at her. "But it wasn't very long, my essay," he said. He put his elbows on the desk and put his chin in his hands in this sad way. " I should have made it longer," he said.

And that was over with. The priest said the school promised to send a letter about the test by May 1st.

So we had to wait a whole month before we knew if Jimmy passed his test or not.

But it seemed like Jimmy didn't think he passed. "I think I messed up with all those abcd's," he said.

Chapter 18

April on our Athabascan calendar is The Month of the Geese, because the geese and ducks and everything like that come back to us then. So everybody goes hunting for them, just tired of dried fish and rabbit we have all winter.

Before the geese come back, that was a bad time in the old days. No game, no fish, no birds. Miss Toby and them told us lots of stories about the starving times. Now we have stores, so we can't starve. Even people had to eat the rawhide on their snowshoes in the starving times. And the insides of willows. Those are sad stories.

In April the snow gets just soft and tired looking and it doesn't sparkle anymore. For awhile at night when it gets colder there's a hard crust on it, so you can travel at night without sinking in. But pretty soon it gets too warm and there's no more hard crust and then it's really bad. You couldn't go anywhere because you couldn't walk on the top of the deep snow. Even with snowshoes. That's when we say the snow is rotten.

The worst part of spring is our rubber boots. You can't wear mukluks when the snow is wet so we have to wear those boots. Those boots are just evil, that's all. They make this really bad ring around your leg where they rub you raw.

And they won't hardly stay on your feet. Every day we'd lose our boots in that rotten snow. I hate that, my legs all scratched up with the ice, and my boots full of cold water. And me and Bertha had to pull little Benny out of the slush I don't know how many times. And we had to dig his boots out about a hundred times.

Everyone was busy getting ready for spring camp. That's when everyone goes out to get muskrats when the lakes thaw out. It's a lot of fun out there, with canoes and all. And you sleep in a tent. Me and Bokko and Mamma went out with Grandpa and them one time when Grandpa was still hunting.

Just five of us would be left in school, and when the others got back from spring camp the ice would have gone out in the river, and school would be over.

And Miss Agnes would go on vacation, and our ginger tom would stay with Luke Simon. And then we'd go to fish camp for the summer.

We weren't sad like last year, because Miss Agnes would be back. But it still wouldn't be the same, without Jimmy. And Bokko would be going away after Christmas.

Even if Jimmy didn't pass his test and didn't go to that school his dad wouldn't let him stay in school anymore. Roger has lots of brothers so he can go to school as long as he wants, he said, but Little Pete might have to leave school, too.

I always wish things could stay the same, but they never can.

It seemed like the days took forever to go by, waiting about Jimmy's test. Every day we'd cross off one of the squares on the calendar. Jimmy was the only one who seemed like he was happy, because he finally could read all the new books. And he did, he read I don't know how many every day. Because he didn't have to study for his test anymore.

It seemed like everyone was quieter than they used to be.

But Miss Agnes didn't seem any different. "Miss Agnes," I said, "how come you don't have a hard time waiting like us."

She laughed at me. "The older you get the more practice you have at waiting," she said. "You know how it is in the summer when it seems like the summer is forever? As if it will never end? Well, when you're older it seems to go by in a second. Time is different depending on how old you are."

I'll have to ask Grandpa about that.

Miss Agnes said we were going to look at mosquito eggs with the microscope. And then we'd let some hatch and we could look at the larva. That's what you call the mosquito when it comes out of the egg. She said mosquitoes are a lot more interesting than we thought. And they were very useful, too.

So after school some of us went out to find mosquito eggs in the grass lakes around the edge of town. Jimmy said we had to bring some of the lake water too, because that's where the mosquitoes' food was, in that water, even if we couldn't see it.

There are black fish in the lakes, too. Plasker got two in a jar to bring back to class. Blackfish are always there so if you really don't have anything to eat you could eat them. That's what Grandpa and them say. But they don't look good and they don't taste good, so you'd *have* to be starving.

And Miss Agnes was right, too. Mosquitoes are a lot more interesting than we thought. She showed us how mosquitoes helped us by cleaning up the water. When they are larva. And then they are another thing. Pupas. And then they hatch into mosquitoes with wings and climb out of their little shell onto the water and dry out and fly away.

And if there weren't any mosquitoes we wouldn't have our birds. Because birds came to us from all over the world to lay their eggs just because we had so many mosquitoes for them to eat. So when we get crazy with them in the summer we should think about how useful mosquitoes are.

But they are so horrible biting every part of you I don't know if I will ever care if they're useful.

We knew all the names of the states now, and some of us knew the names of the capital cities. That's the ones on the map with the star. Like Toledo is the capital of Ohio. But I didn't know all of them.

And we knew a lot of rivers, like the Nile in Egypt and the Amazon, and the Yukon was almost as big as them. It's funny to think that someplace there are children studying geography and they know about our Yukon like we know about their river.

Little Benny was a good reader now and Miss Agnes said next year he could read real books like Selina and Charley-Boy. And next year there would be a new little boy, Marie's little brother. Andy. Marie said he was so excited about going to school he talked about it all the time. And it wasn't for five more months.

It's too bad about what Miss Agnes said, that time goes slow for little kids.

In April Miss Agnes read us *Lassie Come-Home*. About this really beautiful dog. That one was so sad, us girls were just bawling when she couldn't get home to her Joe.

But it came out happy. All the books Miss Agnes reads to us come out happy.

"Miss Agnes," I said, "are there any books that don't end happy?"

"Lots of sad endings in grown-up books," she said. "Remember *Romeo and Juliet*? Couldn't be a sadder ending than that."

Well, even when I'm grown up I will never ever read a book if I know it is sad at the end.

And just when April was over Marie got a letter in the mail from John Wayne. With a picture of him on shiny paper and he had written on that picture.

"To my friend Marie from John Wayne" it said.

I wish you could have seen her face.

Chapter 19

When it was almost time to hear about Jimmy's test the snow was almost gone and there was mud everywhere. Mud is just as bad as the rotten snow, because that mud is just thick and would suck your boots off. Everyone put down all the scraps of wood and lumber they had around the house so we could walk across that mud without sinking in.

Finally it was May first and everyone was waiting for Sam to bring Jimmy's letter. And every time he came in with the mail Sam shook his head. No letter yet.

But after about a week of this one day Sam flew over and he made a big engine noise like he always did, but instead of landing he made another turn around the village and he flapped his wings and flew ziggy zaggy and we all started to yell, because we knew Sam was telling us that he had the letter.

Miss Agnes put her hand over her heart and looked funny.

"Jimmy?" she said. I knew she wanted to know if he wanted to go get the letter, or wanted Sam to come to the school with it, or what he wanted to do.

"Let's all go," he told her, and boy we were glad about that.

So we all went running out of school and a whole bunch of people from town were running up to the landing field. And even Miss Agnes was running sort of. We were all there by the time Sam landed and was taxiing down to us at the end of the field. All out of breath, waiting for the plane to stop.

He had this big envelope in his hand when he climbed out of the plane. He gave it to Miss Agnes and she looked at him hard.

Sam was smiling so big I was worried. Did Sam smiling mean that he knew Jimmy had passed? He didn't know what was in the letter. Maybe he just thought Jimmy couldn't fail.

But I was afraid because of what Grandma said about *hutlaanee*. Maybe you shouldn't do anything to make bad luck happen. Like smiling like you know something good will happen might make something bad happen.

If was Jimmy I would have fainted but he just stood quietly like Miss Agnes. When Sam handed her the envelope she said thank you, and then she didn't seem to know what to do with the envelope.

She held it out to Jimmy but he said, "You look."

So Miss Agnes took the letter out of the envelope. We could see her eyes, reading fast, sliding over that letter, and then she took another page and read that and she pinched her lips together hard and she didn't look up for a minute.

Then she looked up and she handed him the letter to see for his self. She showed him with her finger the part she wanted him to read and he read it and started to smile and looked down at the ground while we all yelled.

Miss Agnes didn't say anything, she just kept her lips folded together like she was scared she was going to cry. When I saw her look like that I almost started to cry myself.

Bokko and Bertha and me went to hug him and then everybody else did, and Paddy hugged him so hard he picked him right off the ground. All the big boys and the men come to shake his hand. They nearly shook it off, and they pounded him on the back something awful.

And Grandma hugged him and called him *googaa*. That means sort of like dear child, which is what you say when you're really happy with someone.

Then we all helped Sam unload the airplane and everyone took a box or something to carry down to the store, instead of waiting for Old Man Andreson to bring the wheel barrow. Sam threw the big mail bag over his shoulder and we all walked toward town together, just happy.

But Paddy looked at Jimmy in a worried kind of way. " You got to go tell our dad." Jimmy looked worried too.

"I don't think he thought I'd pass," Jimmy said.

I got so afraid when I heard Jimmy say that. What if Jimmy's dad said he couldn't go after all?

I ran to Grandpa's and told him what Jimmy said, I was so worried. Grandpa said he thought Jimmy was right, that Henry never thought Jimmy'd pass the test. Grandpa said it was going to be a hard pill to swallow. To know that Jimmy wasn't going to stay home and help him, like Paddy.

But that night we had a big party in the hall and Jimmy's father was there, and he didn't look mad, he looked kind of puffed up about all the hoorah, people patting him on the back and shaking his hand and all that.

Boy I was really glad to see that and Grandpa was really glad too.

Martin Olin and Bobby Kennedy played and Miss Agnes had her concertina and we danced and yelled and acted silly. And even Miss Agnes danced the schottische with Bobby Kennedy, who winked and carried on like he was the handsomest guy in the world.

Then everybody got up to make speeches. People around here really like making speeches and they aren't short, either. And they never can stick to the subject, but always go around in circles, like.

And Jimmy's father got up and gave this speech about how he told Jimmy to get an education, how he made him go to school and wouldn't take any back- talk about it.

Like anybody ever had to make Jimmy go to school.

And how he told Jimmy that he had to pass that test, and if he didn't he'd better not come sniveling back to him because he didn't do his best. "I'm tough on my kids," he said. "That's how you make men of them."

We were all just looking at the floor, because it was embarrassing. Henry always wanted to take credit for everything.

Everyone was just disgusted with Henry. But no one would say anything to him because it wouldn't be good manners. Except Grandma and she just muttered there on the bench while he was talking.

"Big talk for nothing. That's all he's good for, that one. Talk."

But at least she didn't say anything to his face, which I was afraid of.

Jimmy wouldn't make a speech which none of us thought he would. He didn't have much to say, just smiled and smiled.

But I saw him go over to Miss Agnes where she was sitting on the bench. He bent down to say something and she smiled up at him. I think he said thank you.

We all stayed dancing nearly all night. There were lots of little kids just sprawled out on the benches asleep, and some of the grown-ups slept a little while and then woke up and started to dance again. Sam was having a wonderful time, dancing with everyone and even by himself.

"Sam, I said,"how come you were smiling so hard when you brought the envelope. You didn't know if Jimmy passed or not."

Sam winked at me. "Oh yes, I did. I opened that envelope as soon as I got it in Fairbanks. I couldn't wait another minute to find out. Then I just sealed it up again so no one couldn't tell." And he winked again.

I laughed so hard that everyone was looking at us.

That *Sam*.

Made in the USA
Columbia, SC
28 November 2024

47791690R00083